D0098623

# PRAISE FOR *MY SO-CALLED SUPERPOWERS*

"*My So-Called Superpowers* is vibrant, lively, and hums along at a snappy pace. It has a **genuinely warm**, welcoming Saturday-morning cartoon feeling to it."
—Tony Cliff, *New York Times*–bestselling author
of the Delilah Dirk series

"Heather Nuhfer has hilariously and achingly captured what it's like to be in middle school, trying to control the weird things that make you different but also super. And it's impossible not to root for Veronica. **Super real, super fun, and just generally and genuinely super.**"
—Dana Simpson, author of the Phoebe
and Her Unicorn series

"*My So-Called Superpowers* is a super-engaging read with plenty of action, mystery, humor, and heart. **Readers will love Veronica and her adventures!**"
—Terri Libenson, author of
*Invisible Emmie* and *Positively Izzy*

"All Veronica wants is to be special—to be *noticed*—but she gets much more than she bargained for. Readers will empathize with Veronica's quest, and fall in love with this **fun, heartwarming story** about learning to embrace your individual quirks and the power of friendship."
—Rysa Walker, author of the bestselling
CHRONOS Files series and the Delphi Trilogy

# ⚡ My ⚡
# So-Called
# Superpowers

### HEATHER NUHFER

### ILLUSTRATIONS BY SIMINI BLOCKER

**[Imprint]**
MAKE YOUR MARK

New York

# [Imprint]
MAKE YOUR MARK

A part of Macmillan Children's Publishing Group, LLC
175 Fifth Avenue, New York, NY 10010 • mackids.com

Library of Congress Cataloging-in-Publication Data is available.

ISBN 978-1-250-13860-6 (hardcover)
ISBN 978-1-250-13863-7 (ebook)

Our books may be purchased in bulk for promotional, educational, or business
use. Please contact your local bookseller or the Macmillan Corporate and Premium
Sales Department at (800) 221-7945 ext. 5442 or by e-mail at
MacmillanSpecialMarkets@macmillan.com.

Book design by Ellen Duda

Imprint logo designed by Amanda Spielman

First edition, 2018

1   3   5   7   9   10   8   6   4   2

Steal this book if you must,
but you'll get a superpower that is a bust—
slimy, sticky fingers that grab everything in sight,
or hands that detach from your arms to take flight.

*For Paul and E*

# CHAPTER ONE
## LEAST LIKELY TO SUCCEED

I know that a lot of people would say there are worse things than being completely forgettable, but I bet they haven't spent much time at Pearce Middle School. Here the "Ests"—the smartest, prettiest, funniest, and fastest—rule the school. More than anything in the whole wide world, I wanted an Est title of my own. Specifically, "Artiest," which I've been chasing ever since it opened up at the beginning of the school year. (Betsy Monroe dramatically abandoned the title. I'll get to her soon.) This was my dream! This was my destiny! This was—wait, did I hear that correctly?

"Second star to the right and straight on 'til morning!"

Yet again I had been lost in a daydream. This time in the middle of a very important audition during drama class.

"Uh, Veronica?" Mr. Stephens, the drama teacher, said.

I flipped violently through my binder with the script for *Peter Pan* as I rushed onto the stage and it slipped out of my hands and fell to the floor with a loud *THWAP!* I clambered across the stage, snatched up the binder, and scanned its pages for the right line. Judging by the veins popping out of his fake-tanned skull, I was pretty sure Mr. Stephens was about to succumb to a brain aneurysm.

I was so desperate, I just made up Wendy's next line. "Uh, but where are we going?" Maybe I'd get points for improvisation.

The silence that followed clearly meant that wasn't going to happen.

I didn't want to make eye contact with Mr. Stephens. Instead I stood up as gracefully as my body would allow. Then my stomach let out a grumble. Not just any grumble, though; it was inhumanly loud and echoed through the entire auditorium.

"Sorry," I whispered.

"You know there are plenty of junior thespians who would jump at the chance to be auditioning right now?" Mr. Stephens asked. "To be a part of our distinguished Summer Theater Program?"

"I know," I said, finally looking up at him. "I'm so sorry. I really think I'd be great for Wendy. And being at school all summer sounds great. I mean, for theater reasons."

"You are not *professional*-theater material, Ms. Mc-Gowan." He narrowed his eyes at me.

I didn't know what to say, but luckily the crisp pop of foam being broken onstage grabbed Mr. Stephens's attention. Jon, our Peter Pan hopeful, had careened into one of the foam window ledges as he tried to "fly" out the wrong window.

Yep. There's the pinnacle of professional theater.

Everyone else seemed to love Mr. Stephens. He was one of those young teachers who would invite his students to hang out in his classroom at lunch to watch classic movies or have a party to celebrate the solar eclipse. This was my third try auditioning for his summer play, but I had never been invited to do anything other than paint sets or make copies of scripts. I wasn't sure why, but my gut told me Mr. Stephens didn't like me. It was weird. I didn't feel like he hated me, either. I was just . . . not cool enough. What *teacher* gets to decide if you're cool enough? That was a job for the Ests.

"You would've made a great Wendy," someone whispered as I slunk back into my seat.

"Charlie! How long have you been here?" I whispered back, trying not to disturb rehearsal any more than I already had.

"Long enough to see you in a classic Veronica daze-athon." My best friend rested his dirty high-tops on the seat in front of him. "Were you daydreaming about the ice planet Hoth? Were there tauntauns? Did you save Luke Skywalker? That's what I dreamt about last night."

I shook my head. I didn't want to talk about Star Wars, my daydreams, or the play. All those hours of rehearsing Wendy's lines and walking around in a fussy nightgown for nothing!

"You did great when we rehearsed," Charlie reassured me.

"Thanks. I just wish I could have done better here and now."

"Come on, then." He picked a loose strand of his red hair off his jacket. "Art lab is callin'."

"Um, not today. I got permission to . . . do something else." I made my way backstage as quickly and silently as my flip-flops would allow. I'd left my backpack in the prop room.

Charlie grimaced as he followed me. "Ugh. Ugggggh. Not the whole Est thing again, Veri, please! You don't want to be one of *them*."

"You mean the most popular and successful kids in school? Why would anyone want that?"

"The Ests are robots," Charlie said. "I swear. One day the truth will come out."

I giggled as I eased open the prop-room door. It let out a long *creeeeak!*

Mr. Stephens turned around, fire in his eyes. He mouthed, *Not professional.*

Sliding through the door, I found myself in almost complete darkness.

"You looking for this?" Charlie asked, startling me as he shined his phone's flashlight on my bag.

I reached for it, but Charlie grabbed it first and hoisted it above my head. "Can you complete your stupid Est quest without your gear?"

I squashed down my annoyance. An Est wouldn't let Charlie get to her.

Instead, I looked him dead in the eye. "I will be an Est whether you like it or not."

Charlie closed his mouth, and I was quite proud of myself. Shutting Charlie up was a rare, beautiful, mythic thing. A unicorn.

I grabbed my bag, but used too much backswing in pulling it away from Charlie. It flew out of my hands and soared through the air. It was going so fast, I swear I saw a glimmering comet tail trailing behind it. Then it sailed out the door, through the curtain, and crashed into Captain Hook's ship. The *Jolly Roger* teetered for a moment before falling on the stage with a booming thud as drama club wannabes scurried for cover, shrieking overdramatically. The spotlight hit Charlie and me before we could make a run for it. Mr. Stephens stood agape.

"Sorry! Again . . . ," I managed to squeak out.

Mr. Stephens's mouth was forming words, but no sound was coming out.

*BRRRIIIINGG!*

The bell! I needed to be in the gym. Now!

Still unable to speak, Mr. Stephens stretched out a clawed hand and pointed toward the auditorium exit. Being the smart kid I am, I ran toward it, and Charlie followed.

In the hall, I could tell Charlie was ready to give me more of a hard time about the Est activities of the day. Charlie hated the Ests. He thought they were snobs, jerks, stupid, and . . . you know, any negative word you want to shove in there. He was lucky; he didn't want to belong. Charlie was exactly who he was and couldn't be happier about it. Charlie didn't seem to notice if anyone made fun of his red hair or how he was the smallest boy in our grade. He wanted to wear torn jeans and gigantic headphones, so he did. He wanted to speak with a fake British accent, so he did. He was just himself, everyone knew it, and he didn't care. In fact, he seemed to rather like being different from everyone else.

Meanwhile, no one would notice me even if I had a unicorn horn spiraling out of my forehead. Even when I tried to stand out, it seemed like I was permanently average— average height, average weight, average grades, average talent. My brown hair could be curly and wild in the best way one second and curly and wild in the worst way the next. Spoiler alert: the "best way" curly hair rarely correlated with picture day.

I was set on becoming something. Someone. An Est. I had tried everything—and I mean *everything*—to make myself one of them. From studying to be the Smartest (an abject failure on my part) to slapping on makeup to be the Prettiest (I cannot look at photos of myself from that time), I'd failed miserably at each attempt.

Today was it. It had to be. I only had two more activities that might bring out my inner awesome. My plan B was making the volleyball team so I could be the Sportiest, but it was a long shot. Tryouts were during the last period of the day. But right after school was my bigger, scarier, more exciting mission: to get into the Spring Formal Club, or SFC, as everyone called it. Every single member was an Est. Word on the street was that they needed someone to take on decorations. This, my friends, would be the swiftest path to Artiest!

But first, volleyball.

I changed as fast as I could. Keesha Goldman (Fastest) was running tryouts, and I was hoping to get in early and avoid the peeping eyes of Keesha's Est friends who might stop by to watch the new recruits before SFC. I knew I wasn't *that* good at volleyball, and a public mess-up could affect my SFC chances.

There were about ten other girls ahead of me, each rotating into the team and showing their stuff before Keesha marked her thoughts on a clipboard and sent them away.

Behind me, Madison Eckberg and her best friend, Reggie, were whispering nervously.

"Do you think she'll notice?" Madison tittered.

"She better," Reggie replied. "Mine are killing me."

"We shoulda known as soon as she wore them they'd sell out of normal sizes."

I snuck a glimpse. Both Reggie and Madison were wearing some pretty amazing gold sneakers. If you ignored their pained expressions, they almost looked cool. Not as cool as Keesha, though, who'd apparently started Pearce Middle's latest fashion trend. Now, looking down, I realized that I was literally the only girl in the gym without the gold sneakers. My shiny orange high-tops suddenly looked like a pair of traffic cones I'd slipped my feet into. I had spent a whole month filing dental records for my dad to earn enough for them, and I loved them. Or at least, I used to.

I took a moment to envision myself victorious. That's what all the self-help books say to do.

I was up and in place to serve. That was good. It was the only thing I knew how to do fairly well. I lobbed the ball over the net with ease just in time to spot Kate Cunningham (Smartest) walk into the gym and sidle up to Keesha. Was she watching? Nope. They were giggling and not even looking at us! I hustled, determined to get their attention. I hit the ball and let out a loud "Ha!" as it sailed over the net. No reaction from the Ests.

A new player rotated in on the other side and my heart sank.

It was Betsy Monroe. She had been the Artiest our whole lives, and she never let me forget it. It didn't matter if it was a gold star for stick figures in kindergarten or the Pearce County Fair blue ribbon for her watercolor still-lifes of livestock two years ago, Betsy always won first prize and wasted no time telling everyone about my losses. I typically managed second or third or—the kiss of creative death—"Honorable Mention."

This past year she had focused solely on photography, which had afforded me a *slight* break from the constant torture. She was also unceremoniously dumped as Artiest when she came back to school this past year with a major attitude and a new Goth style.

It was Betsy's demise that had inspired me finally to go after an Est of my own. With Artiest up for grabs, my chances were good—except I still couldn't get the Ests to notice me. Hence my focus on every other possible activity in the entire universe.

I did everything I could to avoid Betsy at school—she was still my nemesis—but right now I was trapped. The only salvation was to make an amazing play that both Keesha and Kate would notice and applaud me for. Then they'd announce I automatically made the team, had fantastic hair, and was the Sportiest. Simple, right?

I got into position, waiting to spike the ball and earn my spot on the team, but I could feel Betsy's stare drilling into me. I couldn't look; it would throw me off my game. *Eyes on the prize, McGowan.* The ball sailed through the air, right toward Betsy. This was it. She'd send it back over the net, and I'd be in a perfect position to spike.

I was so afraid to look directly at Betsy that I didn't notice that *she* spiked the ball—until it was headed for my face at about eight thousand miles per hour!

I screamed in a muffled, yet still quite shrill, voice as the volleyball inverted my nose.

Did anyone see? Then I realized how silly it was to think no one would notice me getting pegged by the volleyball, which was literally the one thing everyone *had* to keep an eye on. I wanted to act like nothing had happened, but it was too late. I was falling to my knees.

From my new favorite place on the floor, I felt the sides of my nose. There was some alarming warmth, some blood, but luckily it didn't feel . . . crunchy. I had broken my nose a few years ago when I lost a dare with Charlie that I could swing so high I'd go all the way around the top of the swing set. My sniffer certainly felt crunchy then.

I peeked out from between my fingers. The other girls had formed a circle around me. Some of them were covering their own noses in horrified sympathy while others looked bored, whispered to their friends, or outright giggled. Kids these days, man. I saw a bright flash of light—a camera phone! No!

"I'm fine. I'm totally fine," I lied as I stood up, still cradling my nose. Betsy, of course, was watching from the other side of the net. Kate and Keesha were staring, too.

It wasn't until I moved my hands from my nose that

the blood really started to flow. As my dad often says, "The head bleeds a whole freaking lot." Having a dentist for a dad leads to some gory stories at family dinner.

A small pool quickly formed at my feet as I tried to pinch my nostrils shut. Various shrieks, "ewws," and snarky comments rang in my ears as another camera flashed. Keesha handed me a towel with the tiniest tips of her fingers as I stumbled off the court, leaving a trail of bloody sneaker prints in my wake.

The nurse got the bleeding stopped pretty quickly and assured me it wasn't broken. I tried to explain that I already knew that, but I guess describing your nose as "not crunchy" doesn't hold a lot of meaning in the medical community.

When I got back to the gym, the janitor was just finishing up. He was treating my little bloody mess like a disastrous chemical spill. There was even a yellow barrier tape like cops use to mark off a murder scene. I scanned the room. Such was my Est mania that I needed to know for sure what Keesha thought. Maybe she'd admired my lack of fear?

"Hey . . . you?" Keesha said, spotting me. "I thought you'd be with the nurse?"

"Oh, I'm fine. Totally fine," I lied, trying not to touch the giant wad of gauze taped to my nose. "I just, uh, wondered what you thought about my tryout?"

The instant the words left my mouth, I realized how wrong and stupid they were. I imagined reaching out into the air and grabbing the whole sentence, stuffing it in my mouth, and swallowing it before anyone could hear it. Unfortunately, more words were already flowing. I couldn't stop the idiotic dribble. "I mean, if my face hadn't been there, I would have hit it." I felt my cheeks rise up; I was smiling like a freak.

"Well, yeah," Keesha said, "but your face *was* there."

I nodded stupidly.

"The other players had more plays . . . and less blood. Sorry." Keesha looked back at her clipboard.

"Oh, no, I totally understand." I slowly backed away. "It's cool. It's cool."

I didn't turn away from her until I was halfway out of the gym.

Ugh.

Out in the hallway, I put my head in my hands and did my best to suck it up. Sure, I was humiliated, but there was one more shot at redemption. And I had to nail it. Like, seriously had to nail it, or my whole middle school existence would be completely worthless. This was the end of seventh grade. I had to leave my mark.

In the bathroom, I carefully picked the tape off my bandage and finally got to see the damage to my nose. Yuck. I washed my face and tried to get the crusty blood out of my hairline. My nose was still swollen and red, but at least it wasn't bleeding anymore. I needed to hurry—I had things to do. I quickly changed into my jeans and favorite striped shirt. I stepped back from the mirror, taking a moment to really look at myself. Swollen nose aside, there wasn't much of note. My brown hair lacked the highlights of the popular girls and grew outward in a poof. It wasn't horrible—it just wasn't good. Same went for my height, which was boringly average. I wasn't cute and tiny or gloriously tall and statuesque. I sucked in my belly to see if I could force some curves. I had the extra padding; it just needed to shift to the right areas.

Baby fat or bust, it was time to go. I left the bathroom to find Charlie waiting for me, like always.

I covered my nose with my hand. "Don't even ask."

"I don't need to." Charlie clutched his phone to his chest, a pained expression on his face.

"What?" I cried as I grabbed at his phone.

"Betsy," Charlie said. "Turns out she is as good with a camera phone as she is with an actual camera."

"Noo!" I punched at the apps on Charlie's phone. The picture was everywhere.

"I'm sorry," he said, but a small tick of a smile was starting to show around the corners of his mouth.

"It's not funny."

"No, no. It's not funny at all," he agreed, "but why does stuff like this always happen to you?"

"Just lucky, I guess."

I took another deep breath and tried to compose myself. This was all fixable. It really, really was. It had to be. There was still SFC, the light at the end of my dark, dreary, almost-broken-nose tunnel. I hadn't thought too much about what I'd do if I didn't make SFC, and I didn't want to.

"You're all right?" Charlie was genuinely concerned.

"Nurse said I'm okay," I sighed. "It's the psychological damage that will leave scars."

Charlie laughed. "Sooo, how'd it go other than the messed-up nose?" He gestured to the stream of gold shoes walking down the hall. "Did the gang of metallic feet let you in?"

"Can't you guess?" I sighed. "I'm a loser. Confirmed. For the eleventh time."

Charlie waggled his finger at me. "You listen here, missy. There are better things in this world than a stupid middle school play or volleyball or . . ."

"Or?" I asked, even though I knew the answer already.

He let out a deep, exaggerated boy sigh. "Or some psychopathic, sycophantic mission to make yourself one of *them*."

"Excuse me? I am trying to do something with my life. I'm trying to be somebody."

"An Est isn't a 'somebody,' Veri. It's the big-*est* waste-*est* o' time-*est*. Made for people whose lives peak before they hit twenty. Who bloody cares?"

"Waste of time? But look at the perks I've already gotten." I jokingly showed off my nose.

Charlie ignored me. "You're coming to the mall, right? Ted is working today." Charlie's wide grin covered most of his face.

I looked at my sneakers. "Ah, nope. I still got things to do."

Cue the epic Charlie eye roll. "Like what? Come on. The mall has it all. You can draw the amusing and confusing patrons. Like that lady who wears the pink sweatpants and loafers every day. You love her!"

I crinkled my nose and turned to head back down the hall. "Sorry. Just gotta do one last thing."

"You don't need them, Veri!" Charlie called after me.

I pretended I didn't hear him.

The Spring Formal Club meeting was about to begin. Before I went inside, I peeked through the tiny window in the door. There they were, all those pretty, pretty people. I needed to make myself go in. *Go. Now, Veronica.*

I straightened all the raggedy, loose pages in my sketch-book so they looked tidy. Being prepared is important, so I'd already sketched out decoration ideas and themes for the dance. They had taken a long time to do. Some would say they had taken valuable study time away from my math final. But sacrifices must be made to get where you want to go, right?

I took a deep breath and pushed open the creaky door. The room smelled like fancy perfume and fabric softener. I scanned for an empty seat. Huzzah! There was an open space right next to Mrs. Krenshaw. I could swoop in and be in the semicircle of awesomeness. I slipped into the seat without anyone noticing—and more importantly, without anyone objecting. Time to jump in on the brilliant and meaningful conversation already in progress. . . .

"Gross," Hun Su Nelson (Prettiest) said. "I don't want to be in charge of food again. All that guacamole! Nuh-uh!"

Here it was: an opening. The right words said at this very moment could change the course of the day. Nay, my entire life! I had to be precise, though. Nail it like a laser beam. Like a crepe paper, disco ball hero.

"Uh, I'd be happy to head up decorations," I said, a little more bluntly than I meant to. But hey, I was making my case.

No one heard me. No one even looked in my direction. In the midst of everyone who was anyone at Pearce Middle, I couldn't get a single glance my way. I was invisible, like always.

*Tap-tap-tap!*

I looked out the window behind me to see who was tapping. Of course, Charlie was standing there. He rolled his eyes and gestured for me to come outside. I didn't budge.

*TAP-TAP-TAP!*

The other kids had heard the tapping and were starting to notice me.

"Can we help you, Miss McGowan?" asked Mrs. Krenshaw as she peered out from behind *Hawaii on a Dime*. Obviously, she took her duties as the faculty adviser of Spring Formal Club very seriously.

My face grew hot. "Uh, no. No. Just waiting to sign up," I said.

"Sign up?" Derek Caster (Cutest) guffawed. Then his eyes went wide when he saw my swollen nose.

"Yes?"

Derek glanced at his friends like I was bananas. "Ah, you're only a fifth grader."

"I'm—I'm not in fifth grade," I stammered.

"So you aren't here for detention with Mrs. Krenshaw?" Jenny Marcos (Richest) asked. She looked confused.

"No. I'm here to join SFC. I'm in seventh grade . . . with you guys."

Derek stared at me suspiciously. "Nah. I've, like, never seen you before. There's no way you're in *our* grade."

"I have two classes with you," I mumbled.

Kate rolled her eyes at her friends. "Derek, she was just at summer volleyball tryouts. It's Vanessa!"

"My name is Veroni—"

Jenny cut me off. "Sorry, Vanessa, this is an Est-only club. I thought *everyone* knew that."

It was the way she said "everyone" that really hurt me. Like *I* didn't know because I lived under a rock. In a box there. In the past.

Jenny and Derek shared a smug, "we are so frickin' fancy" look. My nose started to throb again, and I could feel the blood trickling down. Crackers! I needed to get out of there. Everyone was giggling at me. How could I have thought this was a good idea?

"That's enough, everyone," Mrs. Krenshaw said from behind her book. "Those of you who are *not* officially in the club, please excuse yourselves . . . and maybe see the nurse."

I rushed toward the door as I discreetly tried to pinch my nose, but plugging my nose meant obstructing my view. Obstructing my view meant not seeing the backpack on the ground. Not seeing the backpack on the ground made me trip and spill all my dance sketches all over the floor. Spilling all my sketches on the floor made me look like a big dork. Which, at that point, was something I couldn't argue against, which meant I *was* a big dork.

I gathered up the sketches, trying not to cry. The snickers behind me were unbearable! My arms were full of crumpled sketches, so I couldn't pinch my nose. The blood was trickling down, and I saw it *plop* onto the paper. The snickers turned to *"Ewww!* Gross!" as the door shut behind me.

I jammed all the sketches in the nearest garbage can and ran as fast as I could out the front door of the school. Hopefully, I'd get all the crying out of my system before I caught up with Charlie.

# CHAPTER TWO
## HOME IS WHERE YOUR DAD ENDLESSLY PESTERS YOU

"Come on, let's go to the mall," Charlie begged for the millionth time. *"At the Pearcer Maaaall, there's always something new for yoooo-oooou!"* It's the mall's jingle.

I shook my head as we walked down the hill toward my house. Spring had finally sprung in our little town, and everything was lush and green. "No, today was a total disaster. I need to hide."

"You need a distraction. Forget all about this silly Est stuff. Besides, Ted is working."

"Ted? He's getting weirder and weirder, don't you think?"

"We wouldn't want him any other way." Charlie shook

the excess water from a bogged-down crocus as we passed it. "You'll be sad if you miss his unintentional poetry."

"I see what's going on. Your parents working from home again?" That was Charlie's usual reason for finding ridiculous excuses not to go home.

Charlie sighed. "Yeah . . . more research crap. For doctors, they sure don't spend a lot of time with people"—he trailed off for a second before the light came back to his brown eyes—"and they get very cross with me on a regular basis, so you know what I'd call them?"

He waited a beat.

"Doctors without patience."

I snorted and then immediately regretted it as pain shot through my tender nose. "How long did it take you to come up with that one?"

"Just now. I know, I'm *amazing*. Soooo, mall?"

"I just want to go home, see my dog and my dad. Forget I was ever born. You know, the usual." I wadded up more paper towels to shove up my nostrils.

"Okay," Charlie said, abandoning his grand plan. "Speaking of your dad, there's this band tonight . . ."

"I know he'll let you in, he always does," I told him, "but I'll tell him you're going to be there."

Charlie gratefully waved good-bye and left me at my front gate. It was funny to think he was still afraid of my dad. Though, honestly, most people were. My dad used to be in an actual motorcycle gang. Like, seriously. There's this thing in most gangs, I guess, where if you want out of the gang, they have to beat you up really badly. My dad actually went through all that and has become sort of an urban legend for it. They say that after everyone was done wailing on him, he got right up and went out for a steak dinner. Most people take weeks, if not months, to recover. Dad doesn't like to talk about it, but once I did get him to admit it was a true story. It happened long before I was born, but soon after he met my mother.

Now he's a dentist. During the day, at least. At night he bounces folks in and out of the local live music venue, Count's. My pop, Rik, could knock your teeth out one night, then reset them the next morning. A master of pain, some would say, but I wouldn't. I actually know him. He's a secret softie.

I could see his outline through our front door's stained glass window. His hair looked blue through the pane. I wondered what kind of house my dad would have chosen on his own; it probably wouldn't have a stained glass dove flying through a blue sky on the front door. I knew my mom was a hippie. Dad, on the other hand . . .

The house smelled amazing as I walked inside: garlic and oregano, fresh baked bread, and tomato sauce. Now this could wash away the humiliation of my day—if my dad had zero interest in my life. Instead, he asks eighty bazillion questions about everything . . . and one hundred and eighty bazillion questions if it's something I don't want to talk about.

*"Rock on! Forever!"* blared his beloved record player.

Homemade Italian food and classic rock—he must have had a decent day at work.

"I'm home," I called as I put my school stuff in the closet. I saw him in the living room, watching boxing with the sound muted.

"Yo, kiddo!" my dad shouted over the music as he came into the kitchen. Leaning over the sink to wash his hands, he mindlessly dodged the hanging light above it. My dad has the ninja-like instincts of a big dude who spent his life trying not to bump his head on things.

I picked up my little white puppy beast, Einstein. Best pup ever. He wagged his nubby Jack Russell terrier tail as he investigated my aching schnoz.

"Hey, Dad. Smells great in here."

"Lasagna!" he bellowed. "Chuck isn't showing up, is he?"

"Nope. No Charlie tonight."

"Good. I only made enough for an army, not for that eating machine. How was kid prison today?" Dad held out a spoon for me to taste the sauce, but stopped short when he spotted my nose.

"Holy sh—oot! What happened, Veri?" He leaned down to get a better look and cupped my chin with his hand, slowly moving my face around to get a better look. I'm reminded again that we look a lot alike. His skin is a few shades darker than mine, but our eyes are the exact same color: dark brown with hazel flecks.

"You should see the other guy!" I joked. "Seriously, though. I just became very close, personal friends with a volleyball. We're getting married in the autumn. Save the date, Dad; you have to walk me down the aisle."

"When did it happen?" He gave the bridge of my nose a light poke. "Does it hurt?"

"Ouch! Of course, it hurts! I'm not Wonder Woman." I swatted his hand away.

"What *time*?" he asked. "Specifically?" A hint of anger tinged his voice.

"Why?"

"I just wanna know," he said. "As your worrywart caretaker, it's my duty."

"Dad . . ." I could feel the tears welling up again. "After school, okay?"

"Spring Formal Club?" he dared to ask.

A few tears made it out.

My dad drove me crazy a lot of the time, but he was still pretty great. I trusted him more than anyone. I had to. He was the only family I had. I buried my head in his shoulder. He smelled like cigars.

"Yes, I was completely rejected," I said. "After I accidentally hit myself in the face and made everyone laugh at me. Classy. I'm a big old failure."

The timer on the stove buzzed. I released Dad from my pathetic embrace and went to turn off the oven.

He pointed a butter-covered knife at me. "Hey, you only fail if you don't try."

"Where did you read that?"

"I don't know. Pinterest or somethin'. It's crap, right?"

"The mighty words of a soccer mom," I said. "What about you? How much nitrous gas did you use today?"

"On my patients? None." He winked. "My day was good. 'You gotta floss more. See, this is what happens when you don't floss. Here are your dentures because you didn't floss.' Same old, same old." Dad handed me plates. "Now you—spill."

"It didn't work out. I just have to try something else. Again."

"We have a whole attic of 'tries,' Veri," he said, sounding surprisingly down.

I looked at him. "Was Mom popular in school? Or good at anything?"

Dad didn't even flinch. "You are good at lots of things. You definitely get your art stuff from your mom." He chose his next words carefully. "She was popular in high school. We *both* were, but that doesn't mean anything. Certainly not anymore."

He did his fake smile, trying to end the conversation. Dad had never been fond of talking about Mom. Sure, he answered most of my questions, but he answered them *his* way, with only the essential information. Honestly, essential information wasn't cutting it for me anymore. I had lots of questions about Mom. Things I needed—no, deserved to know!

*BAM!* I was so deep in thought, I walked right into the table. "Yeow! Mother—"

With one look, Dad stopped me dead in mid-swear.

"—Hubbard!" I finished strong.

He was not amused.

"You swear all the time," I pointed out.

"I earned the right to swear. I'm an adult. Fill in your own parental wisdom there, but no swearing. Period. It's bad manners for a kid."

"Okay, okay," I agreed, "but as soon as I turn eighteen I'm gonna swear like a sailor."

"As is your right," he said. "Now eat up, matey. I have to go to the club soon."

I waited until the rumble of Dad's motorcycle faded into the distance before I climbed the pull-down ladder into the attic. I hadn't been up there all year, but boy, was Dad right. He had stuffed it *full* with my failed attempts at becoming an Est. It was a mausoleum for dead dreams! Soccer cleats sat next to a dress form and sewing machine. A book on horseback riding propped up a half-built computer. Why was it so hard to be *something*? I just wanted to be cool. More important, I wanted everyone to see how cool I was.

I spotted a familiar light-purple box. It wasn't very big, about the size of two loaves of bread side by side, and I knew every bit of history it contained. Something bubbled up inside me. I couldn't tell if it was fear, excitement, or anger. Probably a toxic mixture of all three. I'd promised myself I wouldn't look in that box ever again. That's why it had been shoved up in the attic over a year ago. But now, I couldn't help myself.

I ran my fingers around the bent edges of the photographs taken when I was too young to actually remember the moment. My mom looked so happy in these pictures. Her red hair bounced. There was a gleam in her eye. She held little baby me so tightly. So lovingly. My little brown hand wrapped around her porcelain finger. Here is where I'm reminded that I also look a lot like her. Or, at least, we share a smile. I didn't actually remember her, but I knew she had bolted not long after these pictures were taken. Why she left was a big mystery to me. My dad's explanation of "things didn't work out" had never really satisfied me. She really seemed to like me in those pictures. So why hadn't she ever picked up the phone or sent a birthday card?

I noticed my mom had the same unruly chunk of wavy

hair that I have. Mine brown, hers red. My dad calls it a "cowlick," which is about the grossest name I can think of.

"Guess I can't say you never gave me anything, Mom."

*Bzzzzz!* My phone vibrated with an incoming text.

**Charlie:** Promise you won't freak

**Me:** Dad didn't let you in? He said he would.

**Charlie:** In. Fine. Not mashed to bits by his mighty man hands.

**Charlie:** Promise me

**Me:** Ooookay. What?

**Charlie:** Blake's back. Saw him on my way here

I took a beat to compose myself. There was this feeling of . . . pain? Panic? Pleasure?

**Charlie:** Hello? Did you implode?

**Me:** Nah, no biggie. ☺☺

**Me:** That was a zillion years ago.

**Me:** I almost didn't remember who you were talking about! LOL ☺☺☺

**Me:** ☺

**Charlie:** . . .

32

**Charlie:** I haven't seen the dude in 1 yr and pretty sure I'd have forgotten him if you didn't talk about him every 5 seconds.

**Charlie:** Not buying it

**Charlie:** And that's way too many happy faces for someone who's telling the truth

**Charlie:** Also, "LOL"? Who are you?!?

**Charlie:** ☹

**Charlie:** Doesn't feel great to be emoji'd, does it?

I flung my phone onto a pile of half-knit sweaters and looked down at my mom box. A drop of blood fell from my nose, splattering on the photo of Mom holding me at my first birthday party. My shirtsleeve only smudged the blood further into the picture. Today was total BS.

I looked at the box in disgust. Mom had forgotten about us. So we should forget about her. Forever this time.

I went to my room and dumped the entire box into the garbage can, then smashed it down with my foot as hard as I could. I felt fractured, like there were tiny shards of every conceivable emotion just floating around inside me. And not to get all pathetic about it but man, Blake? Back?

I should probably tell you about him. As adorable and nauseating as it sounds, he was my first crush, and I've had a hard time moving on.

Okay, okay, I haven't really tried. Our dads have been friends since they were on the high school football team together, so I've known Blake for a long time. Kinda. His dad travels a lot, so he spends a good portion of the year with his mom. If he causes too much trouble when he's with his mom, he is sent back to boarding school, where he's been off and on since seventh grade. It's one of those places where they wear uniforms and all that, and I think it might be worse now that he's in ninth grade. But when he was still in middle school he'd say hi to me in the halls, or (on a very special day) make small talk with me if I was working in the office when he was there to be punished.

A few years ago, before I had a crush on him, there were a couple times he and his dad came over to grill and we raced on our bikes. Remembering it now, I'm pretty sure he let me win. Blake didn't seem like a bad kid to me; just a kid who did "bad" things. What would it feel like to be that way? He never seemed to worry about getting in trouble or going back to boarding school. He just did what he wanted and let whatever was gonna happen, happen. Honestly, he never seemed to worry about anything.

Unlike me.

Oh no, what if Blake saw me with my busted nose? Stupid nose. Maybe it would be better by morning? Maybe I could hide it with some concealer? Makeup hadn't really been my thing yet, but it might be time to dive in. It can't be that hard, right? A few YouTube videos and I'd be a pro.

I grabbed Einstein and climbed into bed. Time for puppy snuggles and time to forget this day ever happened, because there was no way tomorrow could possibly be worse. I started sketching in my notebook, but soon my hand dropped and I drifted to sleep.

Off to dreamland . . .

I could see myself standing in Count's, but it was actually a mix of my dad's club and this hill my dad used to take me to for picnics. Anyway, there I was, watching myself. I was happy, beautiful even. My hair sparkled in the sunshine and was about a foot longer, and the curls looked like perfect ringlets instead of fuzzy poof balls, and it certainly wasn't doing that weird flip thing in the front. Everything was in soft focus, like in a shampoo commercial. I was waiting for someone. Then I saw him.

It was Blake. He had his boarding school uniform on. Not really my favorite, but on Blake it looked good. Everything looked good when you were tall, tan, and had perfectly tousled black hair. Just like in so many other dreams, Blake not only knew who I was, but he also loved me. Madly. I was the *one*.

He embraced me, and suddenly I was back in my body. His gray eyes seemed to see nothing but me. We were about to kiss. I could feel his breath. My pulse quickened. Our lips met, and—

*Wocka-Wocka! Wocka-Wocka! Wocka-Wocka!*

My Fozzie Bear alarm clock made me sigh, stuck somewhere between ecstasy and pain. The best dream I had ever had and a freaking Muppet interrupted it. If I kept my eyes closed a little longer, maybe, just maybe I'd slip back into it.

Pupster Einstein did not agree with this plan. He bounded onto my stomach.

"Oof!" I cried, finally opening my eyes. The bouncy

little pup with his black-spotted ears gave me about a million kisses in 1.2 seconds.

"Little dude, little dude! Good morning! That's enough! Thank you! That's enough! I just had the craziest, bestest dream." I swooned, rubbing the sleep and slobber out of my eyes.

Then my jaw dropped.

This couldn't be real. This couldn't possibly be real!

There were hearts—actual hearts—floating all around my room!

# CHAPTER THREE

## STUPIDPOWERS

Cute puffy hearts with cartoon faces were floating all around my room. I pinched my arm. Then I smacked myself in the face. Yep. Nose still hurts. And those balloons were really there. Or I was crazy. Maybe both.

I delicately poked a hot-pink heart that was about six inches away. It smiled at me and bashfully said, "Tee-hee!"

I jumped back, knocking into one. *POP!*

I gasped—I had killed it. I was an imaginary-creature killer! The one next to it just giggled and said, "Oopsie!"

The dog was staring up at them in confusion. His head cocked to one side.

"They aren't really alive, Einstein," I said, more to reassure myself than him.

Suddenly, Dad knocked on the door. "Rise and shine, buttercup."

"I'm up. I'm up!" I tried to sound normal as I lunged for the door and locked it. "I'll be down in a minute."

The hearts were cooing and giggling as they glided around the room like helium balloons. I put my finger to my lips, silently shushing them. The door frame squeaked as Dad leaned into it.

"What are you watching in there? It's a bit early for anime, don't you think?"

"Uh, yeah?" I replied. "I'll turn it off in just a second."

"Veri? What is that—"

"See ya downstairs, Dad. *Downstairs*! In a minute."

"Okeydokey." His slippers scuttled away on the wood floor.

I looked back at Einstein. He kept bopping one heart in particular with his nose. He obviously wanted to bite it but was being a good boy. I got an idea. If they didn't mind popping . . . Heck, they seemed to enjoy it . . .

"Einstein?" I said, "Get 'em!"

In a matter of seconds, and dozens of "oopsies" later, Einstein and I had cleared the entire room of hearts.

My mind was going a million miles an hour as I grabbed my school stuff and changed my clothes. What in the helloladies just happened? *Did* it really happen? Maybe I was still asleep? Maybe—wait—*maybe* it was a lucid dream? I watched a YouTube video about them a long time ago. A lucid dream is when you can pretty much control what happens in your dream.

"That's gotta be it, right, bud? I'm not starting to hallucinate, am I?" Einstein wagged his tail. I took that as definitive agreement.

"Veronica! I'm heading out!" Dad yelled up the stairs.

I was relieved. The last thing I needed was the Man with a Thousand Questions poking around. "Uh, okay! Have a good day, Dad! Love you!"

I heard his heavy boots clomp to the door. "Love you, too, sweetie!"

*Clomp-clomp-clomp. Clomp-clomp-clomp-clomp.* Motorcycle engine. *Brrrrr!* Gone.

Whew!

At school, I did a stellar job of convincing myself that the morning's incident was nothing more than a bizarre lucid dream. Slowly but surely, the day went on like any other boring school day. For once, school reassured me that I was sane and that everything was okay.

But then again, I had gym class, which was carefully crafted to weed out and destroy any positive feelings of companionship, skill, or hope.

In the dark back corner of the locker room, I could hear Betsy coming by the squeak of her combat boots on the linoleum. Panic is a funny thing. It can give you an adrenaline rush and save your life or freeze you in one spot as wolves rip you limb from limb. I was hoping for the former. I just needed to contain my hair and get out of there before Betsy reached me. I could see my truant hair tie way in the bottom of my locker, peeking out from behind a mini dictionary. I stretched down to grab it. Stretch . . . got it. I raced out of the locker room, brushing by Betsy.

"Where you running off to?" Betsy growled. "Your nose looks better. We'll see how my aim is today." Her eyes were slits, darkened with more eyeliner than my dad had let me wear in my entire life.

I said nothing, per my usual don't-engage-with-crazy-people plan, and went outside to meet Charlie, who was already on the track.

"What up?" he asked.

I looked at Betsy as she came onto the field. "Nothing."

"You arty types are so strange . . . ," he said dismissively before pointing at my swollen, bruised nose. "At least now she has a real reason to pick on you."

True. With my schnoz o' fire, I was prime for the picking on.

"Are you all right?" Charlie asked.

"Yeah!" I replied as brightly as I could.

I couldn't tell Charlie about what had happened that morning. Not only because of the insanity part, but I'd also have to preface it with my Blake dream. Not happening. As far as Charlie knew, I had a normal night and didn't give a flying fig about Blake.

"No, something is definitely off with you . . . ," he said.

I shrugged.

"Did you get new sneakers?"

"Don't you mean 'trainers,' Brit boy?" I teased.

"You just seem . . . shorter or something. I can see the top of your head." He pointed as he spoke. "I can't usually see it."

"Maybe you grew?" I offered.

Before he could reply, our PE teacher, Mr. Smith, shouted from across the track, "McGowan! Weathers! Run!"

"Why do gym teachers call everyone by their last names?" I wondered.

"Maybe that's how they keep themselves from recognizing us as human," Charlie said. "If they realized we were actual people, they wouldn't make us run laps."

"*Weathers!*" Mr. Smith screeched. His face was cherry red.

Charlie flung his arms around lifelessly while lifting his legs up and down. "Yes, yes. I'm moving."

I started running, too, only to be checked from the side by Betsy. I grabbed my throbbing arm and tried not to cry out.

"Ha!" Betsy laughed over her shoulder. "Only nineteen more laps, McGowan!"

"See," Charlie said in his most soothing voice, "she used your last name: future gym teacher."

"Let's just go," I said quietly.

Charlie lit up. "Or we could go tattle. Let's get her in trouble! She deserves it. For. Sure."

"No," I muttered.

"Why not?" he asked. "We have the perfect opportunity! Everyone saw her knock you, Veri!" Charlie flailed his arms around, drawing everyone's attention.

I fought back tears. I was humiliated again and really wanted Charlie to just stop. Now everyone would see me get bullied *and* see me crying. Perfect.

"No, Charlie," I tried to say in a calm tone, but my ugly-cry face was on the verge of making an appearance, plus the high-pitched whine that went with it. "I just want to hide. I don't want anyone to notice me."

With that, I literally shrank about two inches. Now the top of my head barely made it to Charlie's chin. His eyes were as big as moons.

"Whaawoo?" was all he could say.

I stopped running and tried to process. I'd just shrank. I'd just *shrank*. Something was definitely *really* happening. Well, maybe . . .

Charlie had stopped running, too. "Did you see that?" I asked him, not sure if I wanted to be wrong or right about what was going on.

"Schmoo . . . uh . . . yoooou just zipped down a bit. Yeah, I saw that," he managed.

I closed my eyes tight. The hearts this morning *were* real. I had just shrank. I wasn't hallucinating. Crap.

"Considering what just happened, maybe it isn't a biggie, but Betsy is mere moments away," Charlie said, looking over his shoulder.

I saw her coming. Betsy was laughing and joking with another future Roller Derby queen. There was nowhere to go. I felt myself shrink another inch or two.

Charlie pulled me off the track just as I got a parting blow from Betsy. My arm turned red from the hit, and my face was on fire to match. What would happen if they all saw me shrink? Dropping in size wasn't enough. I really, more than anything, wanted to just disappear.

"That's enough!" Charlie shouted after Betsy. "I'm taking you down, Bets!"

Charlie spun around to me, and I saw his face went from angry to majorly confused. I waved at him, but he couldn't see me. In fact, as I held my hand in front of my face I realized *I* couldn't see me. I had gone from shrinking to actually turning invisible.

# CHAPTER FOUR
## BEWARE: HERE BE DRAGON BREATH!

I found myself in Pearce's last refuge: the science hall girls' bathroom. It was a tiny room with itty-bitty windows. It had become eternally gross after Tracy Rollins backed up the toilet with a tampon (allegedly) and flooded the whole floor. Soon after, Tracy transferred to another school due to teasing (allegedly). I had gotten the scoop from my dad. Tracy's mom was his lawyer.

Anyway, that bathroom now came with a stigma. No one who was anyone would *ever* go in it, which is why I hid there. Not that I could actually be seen by human eyes at this point. I still was freaking invisible! And also shrunken. I pulled myself up on the counter, trying to see my reflection, but nothing was there. I ran my hands over my face and through my hair. I still *felt* the same. Since I had disappeared, someone had texted me nonstop—Charlie, I was pretty sure—but I hadn't responded. What do you say? "Sorry! I'm completely see-through right now and so's my phone! I'll text back when I can see my phone again."

I could hear giggling outside the bathroom. No way girls were coming in here, right? I tiptoed over and pressed my ear to the door and recognized that familiar titter: the overly cheery tones of Jenny Marcos.

"I don't see anyone," Jenny said as she pushed the door open. Keesha followed close behind.

They leaned over to check for feet in the stalls.

"Like anyone would come in here now," Jenny said. "After that weird girl permanently grossed it up."

The Legend of Tracy the Tampon continues.

"Speaking of 'that weird girl,'" Keesha said as she opened one of the windows and stretched her arm through it to feel around for something in the bushes outside, "you should have seen her in gym today! Mr. Smith was really freaking out! Apparently, she just took off."

Were they talking about me? Did they actually know who I was?

"I don't know who is weirder, Betsy or that girl, whatever her name is. She's so annoying." Jenny checked her reflection and applied more mascara. "I mean, how desperate did she look at the SFC meeting? It was sad."

"Well, at least she tried, ya know?" Keesha said as she finally retrieved what she was looking for—a pack of cigarettes.

Jenny smirked as she took the box from Keesha. "Sweet."

"Those are really disgusting, by the way," Keesha said.

"Don't be such a stain, Keesh." Jenny slipped the pack into her bag before returning to freshening up her makeup. "I don't do it very often, and besides, I think it looks sexy."

Keesha shook her head. "It doesn't smell sexy."

"Perfume and breath mints." Jenny made a wide flourish with her lip-gloss tube.

Afraid Jenny's hand would hit me, I stepped back and slid on a wet paper towel. I clunked into the sink next to them and hit the tap, turning it on full blast.

"*EEEEEEE!*" they squealed.

Still imbalanced—it's hard when you can't even see yourself!—I staggered sideways, where I smacked into the paper towel dispenser, knocking it off its screws. It clanged to the floor, shooting paper towels into the air.

"A ghost!" Keesha wailed, looking like she might pee herself. Jenny was now shrieking so loudly only dolphins could hear her. She grabbed Keesha and together they ran from the bathroom.

I tried to remember the positives: They actually knew who I was . . . kinda. They may or may not have thought I was weirder than Betsy. Yes, they *did* know Betsy's proper name, but that was to be expected considering Betsy used to be an Est.

Anyway, I needed to calm down. A deep breath or two and maybe I could figure out what the heck was going on. Breathe in, breathe out. It felt good, actually. I took another deep breath and stretched my arms out in front of me. Man, I really needed to touch up my nail polish. It took a second, but my brain figured it out. Nail polish! Nails! Hands! I was coming back into view! I joyfully watched in the mirror as my body reappeared. And I was back to normal size! Happy dance!

Maybe if I just made it through the rest of the day without anything insane happening, things would go back to normal and Charlie would just forget what he saw. It could happen. True, he remembers what he had for lunch on August second, three years ago, but that doesn't mean he can't forget little things . . . like an invisible best friend.

At last it was time for art class. Also known as my happy place. Charlie was sitting at our usual table, staring blankly at a huge hunk of clay.

"Hey, dude," I said casually as I sat down.

He pushed his glasses up the bridge of his nose. "Where were you? You, like, disappeared."

"Disappeared? Ha!" I fake laughed with the best of them. "No. I just had an emergency. A *girl* emergency."

Charlie nodded slowly. True, pulling the girl card was a dirty trick, but I felt if there was a day to use it, today was the day. Most guys will not even attempt to question something labeled as a "girl" problem. Babies.

"It's totally bizarre," Charlie went on. "I thought I saw you shrink out there!" He dug into his clay.

"That's hilarious!" I laughed. Charlie gave me a weird look, but I just waited him out.

"I still think we should have gotten Betsy in trouble,"

he said quietly as he pointed over his shoulder toward the computer station.

Betsy sat there, totally immersed in editing sad photos of lost puppies and abandoned shopping carts (her specialties).

"Oh," said Charlie. "I almost forgot."

He flicked his hand at the bulletin board, and a small hunk of gooey clay flung off his finger and splattered on the board. The sign-up sheet for the student art contest had been posted!

"*Eee!*" I squeaked.

"Better hurry. There are only two slots left," Charlie said as he stuck a googly eye to a lump of clay that was either a monster or a bust of Ronald McDonald. I wasn't sure, but either way I'd tell him it was fantastic.

I didn't move. I mean, I *was* excited for the art contest. But as I thought about it, the winners would be announced a day before the dance. That was too late for me to become an Est, let alone enjoy it, if I won (for the first time ever) and managed to become Artiest.

Charlie gave me a nudge.

I pushed myself up and toward the bulletin board, managing to arrive at exactly the same moment Betsy did. *Gah!*

I motioned for her to go ahead of me. There were still two spots left.

I swear she growled as she slid past. Charlie, ever vigilant, stood up at the table, holding his McMonster ready to use as a goopy grenade should things go awry.

Betsy turned around with a sly grin plastered to her pasty face. I caught myself smiling back. Maybe she felt bad about earlier? Maybe there was a chance we could put all that competition and general evilness behind us? She loafed her way back to the computer terminal and I smiled all the way over to the sign-up sheet. Until I saw Betsy had signed up for BOTH the remaining slots!

"Betsy?" I heard myself shriek. "You can't enter twice!"

"If I'm entering for drawing *and* photography I can."

"Hey! Not cool!" I continued my shriek-fest as heat started to build up in my gut.

"Oh, boo-hoo!" she chided me. "I'm Veronica and I'm so sad that I suck at everything! Boo-hoo! I don't know what I am! BOO-HOO!"

"Quiet down, you two," Mrs. Brannon said, her black bob haircut swooshing as she turned toward us. Our art teacher was a tiny woman who loved realism and classical skill. Before she came to our little town, she was an art buyer for a big museum in New York. Her obsession with clean lines and photorealism didn't mesh well with my style. Betsy's art, on the other hand . . .

"Betsy signed up for the last two spots in the contest," I explained.

Mrs. Brannon rolled her eyes at Betsy. "Why would you do that?"

"I wanted to enter in two categories." Betsy said.

Mrs. Brannon turned back to me. "Slots fill up fast. Why were you so late to class?"

Obviously, I couldn't tell her the truth—that I was invisible at the time. "I just . . . forgot?" I offered.

*"Pssh!"*

Mrs. Brannon didn't believe me. "You're in here almost every day. Don't give me that."

"Are you going to let her take both spaces?" I asked.

"She played by the rules. There isn't anything I can do." Mrs. Brannon shrugged. "Maybe she'll give up a spot out of the kindness of her heart."

The smuggest smile of all time slid across Betsy's face. Pretty sure you need to *have* a heart to use its kindness.

I wanted to yell some more, but the rage boiling in my belly left me speechless. I was burning up.

Finally I opened my mouth to tell her a thing or two, but instead of an obscenity-laden diatribe, a ball of fire spewed from my mouth. It bounced off the bulletin board and hit the coat rack, where all the smocks and aprons hung, setting them ablaze.

Panic took over the room, but all I could do was slap a hand over my fire-breathing mouth. It had happened again—another crazy moment; except this time, *everyone* could see it. But did they see it had come from me? I didn't think so.

The sprinkler system went off as the whole school was rushed out of the building. I grabbed the loop on Charlie's backpack as we lined up on the lawn. We needed to stay together.

As the fire department quickly arrived, Charlie looked at the smoking school, the firefighters, and back to me.

"It was you?" he said.

"It wasn't me! Why would I set art on fire?"

"It. Was. You!" His eyes were alight.

Wait, what? He seemed . . . happy?

But the local news had arrived. I was swept up by local anchorman Stormy Raines (there's no way that's his actual name, am I right?), who gripped my arm so tightly I gasped. The cameraman snapped his fingers and pointed at Stormy, directing him to talk, as he pressed the camera too close to our faces.

Stormy flashed his giant squirrel-toothed smile. "I'm here with a student who saw it all! What's your name, little lady?"

I squeaked out, "I . . . I . . . McGowan?"

"What did you see? I heard you *eyewitnessed* the Molotov cocktail?" Stormy looked at me with great concern.

"Uh, no. No, I didn't. There was just this, like, ball of fire . . ."

"Ha-ha!" Stormy boomed. "Obviously this young girl is shocked to the core! The school has yet to comment, but this reporter feels confident in calling this yet another example of today's youth out of control! Back to you, Chet."

I walked back to Charlie, who was still grinning ear to ear.

"So, you shot out a *ball* of fire, right?" he asked. "That's seriously the coolest thing I've ever seen."

I was very confused. "You think all of this is cool?"

"Very, my curmudgeonly gal pal! You can do things, right? I've seen you go invisible and breathe fire and—and—I mean, what's going on?"

"I don't know! Today, I just . . . think or feel something a lot, and then weird stuff happens. It's happened like twice. Okay, three times."

Charlie was grinning at me like an idiot.

"What's wrong with you?" I snapped at him. "This is the worst thing ever!"

Charlie threw his hands in the air. "Are you kidding me? You have superpowers! This is like an origin story!"

I rolled my eyes. "An origin story is about a super-hero, Charles! With useful powers. *Super*powers, not *stupid*-powers. Besides, this is just a—a thing. A onetime, one-day deal. These whatever-they-are powers are going to go away."

"How do you know that?"

"Because I do," I said in a tone that would tell any reasonable person to stop pressing.

"Yeah, but *how*?"

"Because they have to go away." I looked around to see if any teachers were nearby. "I need to get out of here."

"And go where? Charles Xavier's School for Mutants?"

Before I could smack the ear-to-ear smile off Charlie's face, Principal Chomers gave the all clear to go back inside. The fire had been contained and extinguished with zero damage to the rest of the school. Luckily, I just had to endure only one more period of the day. Not so luckily, I had to spend it working in the school office.

I figured at least everyone would be too busy talking about the fire to notice if something weird happened again. I was right. The office was chaos. I volunteered to answer phones. Lots of parents were calling to make sure their kid was fine. Every kid was fine. Every single one of them. Well, except for me, but I certainly didn't say that to any of the concerned parents. I was beginning to get annoyed with their way-too-similar calls, until I got one that scared me.

"Hello, I'm detective, *ummm* . . . Mulder, calling about the fire earlier today. Has the local PD confirmed a cause yet?" a stern female voice said.

"Um, the PD? As in 'police department'?" I asked.

"Affirmative. As in righty-o," the detective said.

"I know what 'affirmative' means." I caught myself getting annoyed. Who says "righty-o"? *Zip!* A tiny blue electrical bolt shot from my finger into the phone's mouthpiece.

"*Yeowch!*" the detective exclaimed.

*Ahhh!* I had just zapped a detective.

Recovering, she demanded, "I need full names and addresses of all students and faculty who may have seen anything unusual."

"Unusual? Like what?" I stammered.

There was a long pause before the detective asked, "To whom am I speaking?"

"Uh, Veronica . . . ," I said.

"Veronica?" She sounded surprised. "Did you witness the incident?"

Ack! This wasn't good. Evacuate! Evacuate!

"You're br-eak-ing u-p! I-have-to-go-now-bye!"

I clapped down the receiver harder than I should have.

The day was almost done. Maybe I would take a sick day tomorrow, or, you know . . . forever. I watched the clock tick every last little second until it set me free. I ran to my locker. I wasn't even slightly surprised that Charlie had left me a note there, telling me to meet him at his house, "For fun!"

I was convinced he already had a business plan drawn up for our own little comic book starring yours truly.

Pressing the secret key code, I let myself in through Charlie's frosted-glass front door. The front of Charlie's cement-walled, ultramodern house was completely flat, and the doors slid open instead of being on hinges. The house was always cold inside, and there were never dirty cereal bowls in the sink. Everything had its place. It was dead silent today except for the muffled sound of Charlie's stereo upstairs. No wonder he had invited me over—his parents weren't home.

"Charlie?" I knocked on his bedroom door as I swung it open.

"Get in here!" he said, pulling my arm and flinging me onto a nearby ottoman.

Charlie's room looked like it was in a different house. Maybe even on a different planet. The walls were red and covered in posters of obscure bands even my dad had never heard of. The bed was *never* made, and I wasn't sure what color the carpet was because it was always covered in clothes.

"I've been thinking," Charlie began, sitting down on what used to be a patio chair, "today was just a first step. I think we can do better."

"Do better? Charlie, I set the school on fire!" I threw a pillow at him.

"You've got this amazing gift—"

"Gift?"

"*Gift.* And I think we should use it. Save the world. Make some money. I don't know. Something cool," he said.

"Something cool?" I shook my head. "Did you even think about what might happen to me if anyone found out about this? This isn't a cute quirk, like dimples or your stupid accent. This could *hurt* people, including me. If anyone knew about this, I'd be made into a lab rat, not an Avenger! Things don't always turn out awesome."

Charlie leaned back, with a straight face for once. "Yeah. You're right. Obviously, it could be dangerous and scary. I get it." He nodded. "Sorry."

"Thank you," I said. "Now if you had just thought about it for five seconds before—"

"I've been thinking about it since I ditched after fifth period." He stood up and revealed what he had been doing when I interrupted him.

A yellow legal pad had the words "SAVE VERONICA" scrawled across the top and a list below.

"We're going to *cure* you!" Charlie said proudly.

I had no words. I hugged him as tightly as I could.

"See, I think about things sometimes," Charlie said as he gasped for air.

I let him go.

"I'm sorry I was a pain," I said.

"No worries. Women." He rolled his eyes. "They get superpowers and are smart enough not to want them. Le sigh."

# CHAPTER FIVE
## IT'S ALL IN YOUR HEAD

Charlie foraged around on his desk (which was covered in pieces of a model Star Destroyer he'd been building since I met him) and unleashed a purple stethoscope that had "WEATHERS" written down the tube in silver Sharpie.

"Ta-da!" he said with a flourish.

I stepped back. "Dude, there's no way I can be examined by your moms!"

Charlie guffawed. "I would never let those kooks near you! Doctor Charles Weathers in the house!"

He listened to my heart and lungs, but everything sounded fine—assuming he knew what fine sounded like. Our check of my symptoms online suggested that I was under the influence of hallucinogenic drugs or schizophrenic.

Charlie shrugged that off and said, "Okay, we've tried the least invasive methods. Now, let's try something a little more—"

"Invasive?" I shook my head. "No."

"This will be fun. Trust."

I followed Charlie down the meticulously cleaned hallway. The walls were lined with family photos. One was of Charlie and me when we went to the zoo a couple years ago. His mom Lucia was stroking Charlie's hair. He stared, panic-stricken, at a person in a sea-otter suit. His other mom, Daphne, was holding my hand as I tried to lunge toward the otter to hug it. Boy, things had changed a lot in such a short time. Now I was the big chicken and Charlie was the one hugging otters. Or something like that. You get what I mean.

Charlie and his biological brother, Nick, had been adopted when he was a baby and Nick was six. Daphne is British while Lucia is American. Just an FYI, Charlie's accent didn't exist until we started middle school. In fact, he's never even been to the United Kingdom, and Nick doesn't have an accent at all. Unless, when he left for college, he took a cue from Charlie and donned a fake one to impress people.

Charlie inched the door open like it might be booby-trapped. Whoa. I had never been in his moms' home lab before and it was absolutely . . . whoa. Test tubes, microscopes, a centrifuge, and shiny metal tools as far as the eye could see! I went to investigate a massive freezer that was the length of a whole wall. I wasn't really clear on what his parents were always researching, but whatever it was, it apparently required that major experiments could be conducted at home as well as at work. Considering how often Charlie came over for dinner, my guess was that the home lab didn't get a lot of love.

"Don't open that," Charlie warned. "I opened it once thinking they might have hidden some ice cream in there, but it was *definitely not* ice cream."

Charlie directed me to a roll-y chair and unveiled a weird-looking helmet that had tons of wires running all over the outside of it. I was less than thrilled when he placed it on my head.

After the headgear was sufficiently strapped to my noggin, Charlie fired up the attached computer.

"All right, so this thingamajigger can tell what parts of

your brain are currently working," Charlie said, gleefully tapping keys as various bleeps and bloops came from the speakers.

"Y-you don't think it can *read* my mind, do you?" I asked. I couldn't let Charlie know all my thoughts. Or, at least, only about 76 percent of them.

We saw a blob on the screen. Was it my brain?

"I think we got it!" Charlie shouted. "Let's find out what's in your mind, Veronica McGowan!"

No! I reached up to undo the chinstrap.

"Veri, what are you doing?"

"I don't like this," I said, closing my eyes as I wrestled with the strap. *Don't think about Blake, Veronica. Don't think about anything!*

I opened my eyes and a light shot out of them. Straight ahead of me, I could see that embarrassing Blake dream being projected *from my eyes* onto the wall.

"What in the heck is that?" Charlie said.

I shut my eyes.

"Open your eyes," Charlie pleaded.

"No," I gasped. "It shows whatever I'm thinking about."

"A soap opera?"

I tried to think about my dad, my dog, and other "normal things" as I opened my eyes again. Nope. There I was, plucking that really scary, gigantic eyebrow hair that grows right between my eyes.

"Oh, that's unsightly."

I closed my eyes again. "Guess it's not what I'm thinking about. It's what I don't want anyone to know."

"Oh, please," Charlie begged, "just one more. It's only me. Who am I going to tell about your unibrow?"

"No way." I couldn't help but laugh a little, which made it hard to keep my eyes shut. "Can we please just take this thing off? It's making me way too nervous."

"Okay, okay," Charlie said as he helped me remove the contraption.

Once it was safely tucked back into a cupboard, I felt loads better. For good measure, I put on my sunglasses until I was sure this whole projecting thing was over.

"Charlie? You home?" Lucia called from the entryway.

"Hi, Mom! Veri and I are doing homework," Charlie called as we scampered out of the lab and into the kitchen. We cracked open our books just as Lucia and Daphne walked in.

"Hello, Veronica." Lucia gave me a hug. "Whatever happened to your nose?"

"Oh, just sports," I said, waving it off.

Lucia laughed. "That'll do it every time. What are you two working on?"

I said "biology" at the same time Charlie said "history."

Lucia and Daphne shared a knowing look.

"Well, that should be an interesting project then." Daphne gave me a wink.

Charlie turned bright red.

It had become a bit tenser than I liked. Time to split.

I said my good-byes and Charlie walked me out.

"Notice how they didn't even ask about the school catching on fire? It's like they live on a different planet," Charlie vented.

"They think you're self-sufficient, Charlie. That's really cool," I said. "My dad texted me eight hundred thousand times after news of the fire broke. He doesn't think I can handle anything."

"Correction: your dad doesn't *want* you to handle anything. He's a giant control freak."

I nodded. "Can you imagine if he knew about my

powers? I'd never be allowed to leave the house again. Which is yet another reason they gotta go."

"But how do you make them happen?" Charlie asked.

"Make? No making. They just happen out of nowhere, uncontrollably."

"Well, that's just rubbish then, isn't it?" he said. "There has to be a trigger."

"Sure, or I'd be shooting out hearts and lightning bolts while I write English papers."

"Hearts?"

I forgot I had kept that part secret.

"Theoretically," I added. Time to change the subject. Quickly. "*Uhhh*, so let me see . . . I shrank in gym class when I felt scared. And right before the little fire, Betsy blocked me out of the art contest."

"And that made you really, really mad," Charlie added. His face went pink with embarrassment. "Crud. Could I be the trigger? I've been there for all the kerfuffles, haven't I? It could be me!"

Considering Charlie hadn't been in my bedroom that morning, I wagered not. I thought about gym class and how scared I had been of Betsy and how humiliated I had felt to have everyone looking at me. Really, if I was honest, the moment I was most humiliated, I disappeared.

"Charlie, I think I've got it. If I'm angry, I breathe fire. If I'm scared, I shrink. If I'm humiliated, I disappear. Maybe this is all connected to my emotions?"

He nodded slowly. "Could be."

"Now what?" I asked.

"Tomorrow we get a second opinion. And a pretzel."

# CHAPTER SIX
## HEART OF STONE

Much to Charlie's delight, we hit the mall after school on Wednesday and went straight for the pretzel stand. The cheese came out of industrial-sized cans and oozed into the warmer. It looked like a cross between magma and snot. Charlie wolfed down his pretzel, snot cheese and all, before he even handed mine over. Luckily, I wasn't at all concerned with how fresh and hot my snack was. I was desperate for advice on my superpower situation. How desperate? Considering who we were about to consult with, very, very desperate.

Charlie threw away his pretzel wrapper while we waited for Ted to finish reloading the cheese.

I looked at Ted. King of Pretzelasaurus. I couldn't remember when he started working there; it was when I was still little. He was the same age as my parents. However old, he always looked exactly the same: stringy, shoulder-length light-brown hair and a wispy goatee. Ted also had the worst posture I'd ever seen. I wondered if it was from lifting all those cans of cheese.

Pretzelasaurus had been a favorite since we were kids. I used to get so excited when we saw that animatronic dinosaur with the pretzels clenched in its claws. It seemed so gigantic back then, towering over me, smelling like warm dough and WD-40. Now the dino seemed small and rickety.

"How much did you tell him?" I whispered to Charlie. I wasn't too worried about Ted knowing too much, since he'd be hard-pressed to find someone who'd believe him.

"I just told him that you were having some problems and could use his advice," Charlie said.

Hoo-boy. This was going to get interesting pretty quickly. Ted was eccentric, to say the least, and had *somehow* (cough-Charlie-cough) gotten the reputation as something of a fortune-teller among kids our age. One time, Charlie asked Ted what the answer would be to a bonus question on the next day's history test. Ted told him "Albuquerque" and was right. Coincidence? Probably, but Charlie thought Ted had a sixth sense and now regularly asked him about things.

Normally, I thought of Ted as a trippy dude who felt many crystal necklaces and beaded bracelets were the proper accessories for his polyester Pretzelasaurus uniform. That was not judgment I could trust.

Normally.

"Whoa, whoa, whoa. What happened here?" Ted asked when he turned back around and pointed at my face. One of the tassels from his bracelets grazed the top of the cheese.

"Yeah, I hurt my nose." That was as much of an explanation as I cared to give at the moment.

"Ted, Veri wanted to talk to you about something," Charlie said.

"Oh, really? What may I help shine a light upon?" Ted asked as he hopped onto the counter and sat cross-legged.

Charlie smiled up at him. As annoyed as I could get with Charlie, I was amazed that he never seemed to judge people. Or, at least, he never judged weird people. Which, I realized, meant that I was judging people as being weird or not weird. Not cool, Veronica.

I took a deep breath. Was I really doing this? "I've had some strange things happen to me lately, and I wanted to know how to stop them."

Ted interlaced his fingers behind his head. "I know, man."

"You know?" I was both excited and nervous.

"What do you know?" Charlie chimed in.

"Something is cosmically wrong," Ted said to me. "I can see it. Your aura is all jacked up. It's puce."

Defeated, I said, "What? My aura? What does that mean?"

"You got all sorts of things going on in there." He nodded knowingly. "Gotta sort 'em out."

Okay. He was right in a way. "I know that. How do I get rid of all the things?"

"Well, I'd suggest making an offering to the wise ones." He opened one of the cupboards below the register and revealed his own altar-type thing. From what I could tell, it was a mishmash of who he thought of as his own spiritual leaders: Gandhi, Mother Teresa, the pope, and Matthew McConaughey.

Charlie and I looked at each other. Charlie winced.

"Just give him a chance," Charlie pleaded.

I dug through my bag until I found a smashed bag of CheezTwigs.

"Here, St. McConaughey, I think you'd appreciate these the most." I placed my offering below his shirtless picture.

I turned to Ted. "Now what? Is my aura better?"

"You tell me," Ted said with a genuine smile.

"Thanks, Ted, but I really gotta go." I picked my backpack up. "I think my aura is the least of my problems right now. You coming, Charlie?"

We'd started to leave when Ted called out after us, "Veronica, just one other thing. It's important. I swear by the soul."

"I'll be right there," I said, gesturing for Charlie to keep going.

Back at the pretzel stand, I laid it on the line. "Ted, I'm totally out of CheezTwigs."

"This is what I mean. You're missing the grand vista! You need to just be, child. Exist happily in the nature that is you." He folded his hands and bowed toward me.

I stood there for a second and fantasized about him existing in nature. With man-eating bears. What a waste of time.

"What'd he want?" Charlie asked when I caught up to him.

"Nothing. Ted is just . . . so Ted. Whatever that is."

"He's so . . . Zen?" Charlie said. "Yeah. Zen. I think. That's why he's so cool and, you know, emotionally open. It's like he doesn't let his emotions faze him."

A light bulb blinked on over my head. Yes, literally, a tiny light bulb appeared. Thanks, stupidpowers! It danced around a bit until I swatted it away.

"I can see you had an idea, Veri. Spill."

Reluctantly, I said, "I'm not endorsing anything Ted said or will ever say, but do you think his advice was to relax? Be Zen? Do you think that could work?"

Charlie took a bite out of my uneaten pretzel. "Only one way to find out."

The botanical garden was in full bloom. Cherry trees lined the block-sized park, their pink flowers floating through the air. It was beautiful.

I chomped the last of my doughnut and handed Charlie the bag. He was still hungry after pretzels, and I was in charge of making my own dinner tonight, so pretzels and doughnuts it was! He could entertain himself with the rest while I tried my experiment.

I had my dad's noise-canceling headphones ready to go, and I'd synced up a series of guided-meditation MP3s that would hopefully squelch the madness within. Maybe, just maybe, if I chilled out enough, I'd be able to brush off all these feelings and their related stupidpowers.

The soothing Australian accent of a man named Randu filled my ears. He directed me through a series of deep-breathing exercises to let my thoughts come and go as they pleased. I started to feel a little zoned out. I couldn't feel the breeze anymore, or the grass under me. My limbs felt heavy. Impossibly heavy. I could stay in this position, just like this, forever . . . I was so at peace that—

"ACK! UGH! What is—" I sputtered, thrust out of my Zen state.

Charlie stood in front of me, looking terrified and holding one of his nasty socks in front of my nose.

"Gross! What the heck are you doing?" I cried, wrinkling my nose.

"Look!" he said, pointing to my crossed legs.

"Oh, fudgebuckets!" I said.

My legs had turned to stone.

"Your *whole body* was like that a second ago!" Charlie said. "You were a living statue. It really freaked me out, so I had to give your system a shock—of the foot-odor kind."

Looking down, I realized I was still stone from the shoulders down. I tried to wiggle my limbs free, but there was no give. This was going to take some time. That was when I noticed Charlie looking over his shoulder.

"What?" I asked, suspicious of his very suspicious behavior.

"Um, ah, can you move yet?" he asked, scratching his eyebrow the way he always did when he was nervous.

I could feel my legs now, but they were still gray and immobile.

"Not yet. Why?" I had a feeling I really didn't want to know.

"Well . . ." Charlie fake smiled. "It appears Blake is headed this way."

"No. No, no, no, no, no." I used every ounce of concentration I had to force my legs to move, but it didn't work. At this point, it would take something like a crane to move me. If I couldn't get up, Blake was going to see how freakish I was!

"Relax!" Charlie said. "This guy was nice to you once last year! Who cares what he thinks?"

"You don't understand."

"That's totally accurate. I do not understand."

"At stupid band camp, everyone was so mean to me, Charlie. You know how tone-deaf I am! He was the only one who would rehearse with me. He didn't care."

Blake was getting closer.

Naturally, I panicked. "Charlie! What do I do, what do I do?"

Charlie shrugged as he took my headphones off. "I guess Dream Man needs to learn the truth. Apparently, he's cool enough to take it."

Blake would spot us any minute. In a moment of brilliant yet stupid inspiration, I came up with the only solution.

"Put the doughnut bag over my head," I whispered.

Charlie gently shook the bag. "Dude, there are still two doughnuts in here."

"I don't care. Shove them in your gullet and put the friggin' bag over my head! Please!"

"Ten wut?" Charlie asked, mouth now packed full of confectionary delight.

I didn't have time to explain; Blake was just a few yards

away. Charlie yanked the bag over my head, showering my freshly washed hair with crumbs and sugar.

I could hear Blake's footsteps getting closer. I couldn't see what was going on, but here's what I heard:

BLAKE:

Hey, Charlie! What's up?

CHARLIE:

Oh, wofthin', dwood.

BLAKE:

Really jamming on those doughnuts. What are they? Powdered sugar?

CHARLIE:

Wep.

Oh no. All the powdered sugar was making me need to sneeze. I felt it brewing. My eyes started to water. Come on, Charlie, move it along!

BLAKE:

(laughs) And up to some early-morning vandalism? Right on, man. Is that statue new? I've never seen it before.

CHARLIE:

Mwusta gwhot it while yoo were away.

BLAKE:

True. Just remember, doing stuff like that is
what got me sent off to boarding school.

CHARLIE:

(big gulp) Noted.


I couldn't hold it in anymore. A delicate but audible
*achoo!* radiated from my paper bag.


BLAKE:

What was that?

CHARLIE:

I, uh, had a little sneeze there. That's all.
Allergies. Outside. All that.

BLAKE:

Bananas! It sounded like it came from your
little stone friend!

CHARLIE:

Ah, yes! Ha! How funny and unlikely that
would certainly be.

I cringed. Charlie always got super proper when he was nervous.

BLAKE:

Uh, okay. See you, man.

CHARLIE:

Indeed, sir.

BLAKE:

Man.

CHARLIE:

Man?

After the sound of Blake's footsteps were out of range, Charlie whipped the bag off my head.

"Oh dear." Charlie wrinkled his nose at me. "It appears you've been attacked by the Sugar Plum Fairy."

We had to hang out for a while until my legs allowed me enough movement to get home. I spent the rest of the day trying to recover.

"You're stuck with these powers, right?" Charlie was skipping along in sheer annoying merriment. "So why don't we use them to our advantage?"

I sighed, dragging my still-heavy legs down the English department hallway the next morning. "I don't have any control over them, remember? I just need to wait for them to go away."

Charlie replied, "What if they're permanent?"

I stuffed my books in my locker, trying to avoid dealing with the question. "It might just be some . . . puberty thing." I nodded my head, agreeing with myself.

"Puberty?" Charlie laughed. "I guess that puts my worrying about facial hair in perspective."

He playfully smacked my shoulder. I couldn't help but laugh.

"Come on, study hall," Charlie said.

"Not me. I got called in for an appointment with Doctor Dirk."

"*Eesh.* What did you do to get slapped with a guidance counselor chat?"

"Nothing," I said, searching my memory. "I mean, nothing that he would know about. I hope."

Doctor Dirk Phillips was an old-school hippie-type

dude who wore velvet vests and once caught his office curtains on fire while burning incense. Still, fire hazard aside, he was pretty harmless, so I wasn't too worried about whatever he wanted to talk about.

I headed to the counselor's office and had to wait a few minutes. I watched the school secretary, Mr. Fenkel, search for his lost car keys, and was mildly fascinated by just how many tissue boxes were on his desk. From what I could see, the desk itself may have been made of tissue boxes.

"Miss McGowan?" Mr. Fenkel finally droned through his cottony white teeth. "You may go in."

I smiled as I opened the door, trying to start this off smoothly.

"Veronica, I'm your new guidance counselor." An angular woman in a stiff navy-blue business suit leaned over her desk and shook my hand. "Ms. Watson."

I felt the corners of my mouth fall. "Where's Doctor Dirk?"

"Doctor *Phillips* was reassigned," Ms. Watson said as she sat down. "I thought it would be wise to get some face time with everyone involved in the fire the other day."

I leaned way back in my chair, hoping to look relaxed. "Me? I'm totally fine. All is well."

"You weren't traumatized?" Ms. Watson leaned forward.

My mind raced. Traumatized? What did she know about it? Could she tell something was up just by looking at me?

"A lot of your classmates are having a hard time dealing with the fire," she said. "They feel unsafe."

I nodded. "Understandable, for sure. It was . . . scary."

"Why did it scare you, specifically?" she asked.

Don't dig yourself in deeper, Veri. "Well, middle school is generally scary. There's no need for a fire to make it scarier. I guess."

"You're frightened on a daily basis?" she asked as she rummaged through her desk drawer. "Show me on the Emotion Wheel," she held out a rainbow circle of cardboard. Each color of the rainbow had an emotion written on it. Red was anger, blue was sad—you get it, right?

"No disrespect to the cardboard, but I think I should probably get back to studying."

She pretended she didn't hear me. "Do you feel that you're different from the other students?"

"Uh, no? I think I'm pretty average."

"You are Rik and Rebecca McGowan's daughter, correct?"

"Uh, yes?"

"We may need to schedule a parent-teacher conference," she said.

"With my dad? Sure, if you wanna go down that road. He doesn't handle authority that well though, so . . . ," I drifted. "My mom has been gone a long time."

"And you don't know her whereabouts?" She pressed, raising an eyebrow.

"No. Why, do you?" I regretted the words as soon as they left my mouth. The level of snark in them was probably felt on the moon. But who did this lady think she was? You can't just ask a kid such a loaded question.

I smiled, but as I thought about my mom I could feel tears welling up.

Ms. Watson must have noticed, because she became very flustered and started rifling around in her desk. "Oh, shoot. I thought he left some tissues . . ."

I looked away and wiped my eye with my sleeve. "It's fine," I said. "Just don't make me use the wheel." Although come to think of it, that Emotion Wheel might come in handy to assess upcoming superpower outbreaks.

Not that I'm big on the whole stealing thing, but this was a little hunk of cardboard. I bet she had a zillion of them. I stuffed it in my backpack just as Ms. Watson produced something else from her desk drawer. Ooh! She had chocolate!

"Can I take two?" I asked. "Charlie will want one. He's big on eating lately."

"He's the red-haired Caucasian male? Approximately five feet three inches?" she asked. "He was with you on the television."

I stopped halfway through the bite of my mini Mounds. "You saw me on the news?"

"Yes, that's why I was particularly interested in talking to you. You seemed so . . . so affected, I guess."

"I'm fine," I said. "But thanks for checking."

"Righty-o!" replied Ms. Watson, smiling at me as I got to my feet.

The door shut behind me. I was chewing the rest of my chocolate but didn't taste it. I was lost in thought. The detective on the phone had said "righty-o," too. Maybe it was a new thing to say if you're an adult trying to not sound like an adult?

I threw the candy wrapper in the trash, but my arm wasn't moving very fast. I looked down to see several thick, smooth ridges on my wrist. I slid my hand over the skin there; it felt smooth and hard. The weird armor there was expanding! And it was green! It looked familiar, like my old turtle, Darby.

Holy cow, Ms. Watson had really gotten to me! I was growing a turtle shell!

It was time to employ my favorite old sweatshirt. It may have seen better days, but a few rips were nothing compared to its ability to conceal my new shiny green shell. I zipped it all the way up and shoved my hands in the pockets.

As I headed out the door, I was unlucky enough to trip over Betsy, who was on one knee taking pictures of the Eisenhower statue in the front quad.

"McGowan!" she grunted.

"I'm really sorry," I said. All I wanted was to get out of there before anyone noticed how hard and lumpy I was.

"You ruined my shot!" She grabbed my shoulder. I tried to wriggle away, but instead of feeling her vise grip of a hand, I felt . . . nothing.

Betsy had grabbed my shell!

"What the heck?" Betsy retracted her hand and gave me a befuddled, slightly grossed-out look.

"*Uhhh*," I stammered as I pulled my sweatshirt tight around my neck, "I-I've been working out!"

I broke into a run—Mr. Smith should've seen me!—and headed home. I needed to get rid of these powers.

Luckily I had an idea—but it was gonna get messy.

# CHAPTER SEVEN
## EMOTIONAL RESCUE

Back at my house, I told Charlie about my meeting with Ms. Watson.

"It's kinda trippy," Charlie said as he spun the Emotion Wheel I had "borrowed" from Ms. Watson. "What are we doing with it?"

I joined him on the floor. "I was thinking that maybe if I went through *all* the emotions, I could get rid of my powers. You know, purge them. All at once."

"That, my friend, is a very smart idea!" he said.

"Thank you. Listen, Charlie," I said carefully, "this is probably gonna be pretty intense. If you don't want to hang around for it, I totally understand."

"What? No way! I am staying."

I picked up the Emotion Wheel and pondered where to start.

"How are you feeling now?" Charlie asked. "Maybe we should start on the easiest?"

That seemed logical, for sure, but figuring out how I was actually feeling right now? Man. I was feeling . . . everything. I was anxious and excited and terrified and annoyed and . . . hungry.

"Chips," I said, jogging over to the cupboard.

"As much as I truly *feel* that 'chips' is a valid emotion, I can't seem to find it on this wheel," Charlie said. "Do you have anything in a 'happy' or 'confused'?"

We laughed and for a second, everything seemed normal, like it used to be. Just me and Charlie, eating chips in my TV room.

"So, let's get to it?" I pushed.

"We don't have to do this," he offered. "We can just hang out. Eat chips. Or, rather, crisps." Charlie could tell I was nervous, and it was tempting to try to forget about my powers, but they'd still be there. I'd still be turning into stone and burning buildings down.

"No, we can't pretend this isn't happening to me," I said. "Pick an emotion, any emotion."

Charlie closed his eyes and waggled his finger in the air before smashing it down on the wheel.

"I chooooooose you!" he yelled as he opened his eyes. "*Hmm.* Grief. That's an interesting one."

"Okay," I said. "I just need to think of things that I've lost."

I closed my eyes and focused.

*Crunch!*

"Charlie, that isn't helping."

"Sowwy," he said through a full mouth. "Think about griefy things, please."

"I'm trying." I sighed. "Do you have to keep eating right now?"

"Yes. I'm a growing man," he said, "and I think I'm about to have a growth spurt." Then he got serious. "How about the, um, loss of your mom?" he tentatively asked.

"I didn't 'lose' her; she left," I grumbled.

"Okay, Fancy-Pants Feelings Lady, what about the whole loss of your normalness?"

I thought about that for a moment.

"Holy baloney," Charlie whispered. "You're slowly turning black and white." He was still whispering.

"Okay, maybe that means it's working?"

"*Shhh!*"

I tried to focus on my loss, but it was hard. I kept thinking about Charlie shushing me, and then, of course, I heard:

*Crunch, crunch, crunch!*

I stifled a giggle and opened my eyes.

"Ha!" Oh man, I *was* black and white. I looked like an old cartoon. But now that I was laughing, something even stranger was happening. Every time I laughed, a tiny cartoonish black-and-white bird flew from my mouth and started flying crazily around the TV room. Soon there were a bunch of them, dive-bombing everything and leaving splashes of birdy mess—and their poop was in Technicolor—all over the beige shag rug.

"No, no, no!" I cried as I took cover under the coffee table. Charlie was faring worse than I was—he was being pelted left and right. He was holding a coaster over his head, but it wasn't helping. *Ewww!*

"Veri!" he shouted, dodging the winged warriors. "You need to get control of your power back!"

"Get control of my power back? What are you, a motivational speaker?"

"No, change your emotions! Make them disappear!"

Not a bad idea. *All right, Veronica, you are strong, you are powerful,* I told myself. I didn't really feel it, mainly because I was hiding under a coffee table while trying to ignore Charlie's shrieks.

Okay, being powerful meant being strong. I thought of all the times I had been physically strong. I could carry *all* the groceries into the house in one trip if I wanted to. That was pretty freaking tough. My arms were beginning to feel warm, and they slowly puffed out from my body. I was feeling quite powerful, and my muscles seemed to be growing in response.

I did it. I actually controlled my powers. I flexed one of my gigantic muscles. So cool!

"Veri!" Charlie squealed from behind me.

I turned to look at him. He was still flailing on the ground as little birds pecked at him and pooed all over. Our floor looked like one of those splattery paintings at the museum.

Wait, it hadn't worked? Suddenly, I felt really helpless.

This was a disaster, and I had caused it all with my uncontrollable stupidpowers.

I reached out to him from under the coffee table, but I was stuck. My gigantic arms had wedged me tightly between the table legs. I grabbed a leg with my one free hand, and it immediately snapped like a twig between my fingers. The table toppled over onto me, and I pushed it off. It cracked apart.

"Crackers! Who knew that table was so weak?" Or was it me? Was I too strong? I gingerly picked up one of our TV remotes with two fingers; it smashed into a shower of batteries and buttons. I touched a throw pillow with one finger, and it exploded, spreading stuffing everywhere. The birds had quieted down; they were now darting between corners of the room, up near the ceiling, wary.

"Charlie!" I yelled, reaching out to him.

"No!" He crawled away from me. "Don't touch me! You'll accidentally mangle me."

Charlie made it out of the room and shut the door behind him.

"Not that I don't love you dearly," he said from the other side, "but I'm just going to wait right here until things . . . chill."

I looked around. The room was absolutely trashed. I carefully sat down on the floor, trying not to destroy anything else. I took a couple deep breaths and closed my eyes. I didn't know what to think—except that I needed to stop trying to force these feelings and the powers that came with them.

Soon the squawking stopped, and I felt birdy feet on my shoulder as they landed on me. My arms had started to shrink back down.

"Yo!" I heard my dad bellow as he came in through the garage. Einstein's nails clicked on the wood floor as they got closer.

"Uh, hi, Mr. McGowan!" Charlie shouted, trying to mask his fear with friendliness.

"Call me Rik, I keep telling you. Where's our girl?"

"Um, uh. That's cool you take Einstein to the office with you." Charlie was stalling. "He seems more like a work-from-home kinda pup to me."

Popping sounds filled my ears. Apparently, even the dive-bombing birds didn't want to face my dad's wrath. They had destroyed themselves, along with their mess. The wreckage I'd caused, on the other hand, was still there.

The door squeaked open.

"Veri! It looks like freakin' WrestleMania in here!"

Like most benevolent dictators, my dad doled out a swift and fitting punishment. Charlie and I were told to clean up with the promise that he and I would have a "talk" once we were done. The only bit of luck on my side was that Dad couldn't ever figure out the remotes, so missing one meant nothing to him. I was fairly sure he wouldn't even notice.

"So, what do we do now? What's next?" Charlie asked.

"I don't know. I certainly can't have anything else like this happen. I mean, none of our experiments have been successful, like, at all."

"I wouldn't say that . . ." Charlie looked around the room. "Maybe just keep cataloging your emotions and their corresponding powers in your sketchbook? Tick them off on the Emotion Wheel? Maybe they will still go away when you hit them all. It was a good idea, Veri."

I reeled. "That's about a zillion emotions. That could take years."

"You're a teenager—hormones will prevail. It'll take about a week, tops,"

"Hardy-har-har," I said.

"Got a better idea?"

I sighed.

Once the mess was cleaned and Charlie went home, I tip-toed upstairs to Dad's room and gently knocked on the door. Time for the Dad Inquisition. I had no idea what I was going to say to explain away my stupidpowers.

"Dad?" I called out as tentatively as possible. He didn't answer, but I could hear him talking inside. He sounded mad, which wasn't unusual if he was on the phone. He hated the phone. This time he sounded angrier than I had ever heard him, though. I pressed my ear to the door.

". . . well, there is nothing to say because there is nothing going on, okay? Period."

A second later he let out a heavy sigh and swung open the door, leaving me standing there like I had been eaves-dropping. Which was mostly true.

"Hi," I said sheepishly. "Prisoner McGowan is here for her sentencing."

Dad shook his head. He looked sorta sad. "Just go to bed, Veri. It's fine."

Fine? Wait, what? "Is everything okay, Dad?" Now I was worried. No questions, no explanation, no further punishment? This wasn't how Dad acted. Ever.

"Yeah, yeah," he said abruptly and then gave me a big hug. "You cleaned up the mess; don't do it again."

"I won't," I said as I watched him walk down the stairs. I had never seen my dad so out of sorts and I didn't like it. Whoever he was on the phone with had gotten under his skin.

I scratched my head as I pondered the morality of what I wanted to do now. Dad had left his phone to charge in his room. It wouldn't hurt to take just a quick look to see who he was talking to. Maybe I could help. I typed in his phone password (it was my birthday; I had programmed it for him) and looked at recent calls. The last entry didn't have a name, just a number. The rest were either me or work or his gray-bearded biker buddies. I added the number to my contacts and went to my room. A quick Internet search and I had a lot of results for that phone number, but to get a name or address, I had to pay a fee. With a credit card. Come on! Thus ended my Internet sleuthery for the night. I had another day of stupidpowers to contend with tomorrow; I needed some rest.

"Veronica!" Derek's smooth voice cut through the chaotic din of everyone fleeing school as fast as possible.

He also startled me. I wasn't used to hearing anyone except Charlie and teachers shout my name at school. A metal horn, like the one I used to have on my bike, popped from my head, blaring *Awoooa! Awoooa!* I smacked it into my locker and slammed the door before Derek could see what had happened.

"Alarm on your locker?" he asked, raising one eyebrow.

I tried to look casual and leaned back against the locker. The alarm was trying to escape by bashing itself repeatedly into the door.

"No. Just a crazy ringtone."

"Do you need to answer it?" Derek asked. Phones were really important to him.

"Nah, it's probably just . . ." My mind had gone blank. Did I know anyone? This was taking too long. Just say a name! ". . . my mom," I blurted out. I could tell my face betrayed me.

"I see." Derek took a small step back. "Anyway, I just wanted you to know that Keesha can't be on Spring Formal Club now."

"Oh, that's too bad," I said. "What happened?"

Derek furrowed his brow, clearly not sure what to say. "Jenny, um, I mean, *we* decided she needed to go. That's all I can really say."

I nodded like I knew exactly what he meant. I had no idea what he meant. (*Awoooa!*)

"I mean, we were fine without Betsy, but having *two* open spots is just too much extra work, you know?" Derek said. "So, like, you want in?"

"Me? Really? You want me?" My attempt at laid-back? Not so good.

"Yeah . . . um . . ." He delicately picked through his white messenger bag until he retrieved a smoothed-out, blood-splattered sketch. It was one of my dance ideas!

"We found these and thought, you know, why not? Apparently, you're cool with the work and stuff. So, meeting after school, 'kay? At Café Blasé." Derek was already walking away.

"Yes!" I said before I really thought about it. Then a certain *Awoooa!* brought me back to reality. Oh my gosh.

Oh my gosh! Did this really happen? Finally I'd be part of the SFC! I was so excited I didn't even care about what could happen. Powers or no powers, I had to do it. I mean, this was all I ever wanted!

Still, the only thing harder than having stupidpowers would be convincing Charlie that I should be in the SFC.

"That's a rare sight," Charlie said.

"What?" I asked, even though I already knew what he was talking about. I was smiling so hard it was beginning to hurt.

"It looks like your teeth are trying to escape your face. Tell me, what do your shiny human teeth know?" Charlie demanded as we walked.

I started skipping. I have no idea why, but I just went along with it. That's how happy I was.

"I, Veronica McGowan," I started, "am now a member of . . . *the* SFC!" I stared at Charlie expectantly.

He shook his head. "No. No, no, no. What about your superpowers? Wouldn't you rather investigate those with me instead of hanging around those bozos?"

I stopped skipping. "Well, yeah, *but* it's also the only thing I have ever wanted, and it's happening to me now. *Now!* How could I possibly refuse? Why can't you just be happy for me?"

"Happy? Happy?" He grabbed his hair.

"Yes! That's what friends do. They are happy for each other when good things happen."

"You and I have a rather different definition of friendship," Charlie said. "As your friend, I believe it's my responsibility to look out for you, no matter what. Even if you don't agree, or don't like it, or grow some scary monster shell."

"You saw my shell?" I pulled my sweatshirt up tighter around my neck.

Charlie gasped. "You had a shell?"

He was so excited, I couldn't help but laugh and, of course, no longer be annoyed.

"Ah, the magic of friendship!" I waved my arm in the air grandly.

To our surprise, a small rainbow arced from my arm.

"Holy cow! I controlled that!"

"You did?" Charlie asked.

I wasn't sure, but I didn't feel *out* of control like I usually did.

"I-I think so. Maybe that means it's almost over."

"For your sake, I hope so," Charlie said, "but for super-powers' sake, I hope it isn't."

I arrived home feeling far more positive than I had in quite some time. Things were finally going my way. And the next stop was everything I had ever wanted!

If I didn't accidentally set the SFC on fire with my stupidpowers.

# CHAPTER EIGHT
## EAT YOUR GREENS!

Café Blasé was like a lot of things in our town—new, yet somehow old looking. Opened by someone who obviously had their glory days back in the mid-1990s, like most of our parents, it was a time capsule dedicated to round furniture, primary colors, and *Friends*. Still, it was the best we had. Our only other option was the local Parkin's Family Diner. There we would, undoubtedly, be given colorable place mats and children's menus. At least Blasé's owner, Frank, had no qualms about selling overly sweetened coffee drinks to kids. Er, young adults.

I had rushed to get my things and plow out of school so I would have a few minutes at home to compose myself and check my nose and swipe on some lip gloss. My speediness seemed to pay off. As I got close to the door, I could see there were no other SFC members in the café yet. But there was someone there I really didn't want to see. Not today, at least. Or, more aptly, not until I felt and looked and acted like a totally different person. An awesome, beautiful person who could compose complete sentences.

Blake.

This time I didn't have a doughnut bag over my head, so I could actually see him. His hair was different, and better. Didn't hang so much in his eyes.

Hooray! A rescue! The whole SFC had arrived in a single drove. I could just slide on in with them. If Blake even noticed me (unlikely), I would look wildly popular and possibly even normal. Not at all like a girl who spends her evenings struggling with nonsensical, useless superpowers.

"Veronica. You made it," Jenny said in a more factual than pleased tone.

"Sure did!" I couldn't help but sound overly zealous as I held the door for everyone. "Excited to get working!"

We passed the pastry case in a huddle. I stayed closer to Kate than either of us was comfortable with, but we would have to endure. Blake was sitting only a few steps away at the counter, and I needed a human shield.

"Yuck," Hun Su said under her breath when she spotted him.

I knew the truth, though. I could see a familiar look in her eye. Forbidden fruit, baby. If there were polar opposites in the world, Hun Su and Blake were certainly them. Hun Su was petite, with the longest, shiniest black hair I'd ever seen. She was amazing with makeup, even though she didn't need it. She was somewhat loud and talkative, which some people called bossy, but she wasn't. She just had confidence in her opinion.

Blake's style, on the other hand, wasn't so much "fashion" as whatever he rolled out of bed in. My dad calls it "grunge." Anyway, I could see the appeal in dating the "bad boy" while also totally irritating one's parents.

Blake turned at exactly the wrong moment. We locked eyes. A half-crooked smile crossed his face. It took a few seconds before I realized I was smiling back like a complete and total idiot.

I was sure that at some point in my life I had known words. Lots of words, even, but at the moment, I could find none. So I just kept walking and sat down with the rest of the SFC and pushed Blake out of my brain as much as possible. I had things to do. This was it! This was the good stuff—the beginning of my new life as an Est. Artiest. I took a few notes in my sketchbook and nodded a lot. Proof that I was completely on board.

The presence of Betsy with a camera couldn't even ruin my high. Besides, she was there to document the SFC for the yearbook, and the SFC now included *me*. I would be right in there—smack dab in the center—for the two-page spread. Although Betsy was evil enough that she would probably find a way to cut my head off in the pictures. I crouched down so I was at the same height as Hun Su and leaned closer to her. Even Betsy wouldn't dream of cutting out Hun Su.

Close up, I noticed Hun Su wasn't really paying attention to us at all. She was looking off into the distance. I followed her gaze. I shouldn't have. She and Blake were deep into a flirt of epic proportions. Their eyes would lock, she'd look away, and then he'd look away. Then they'd look back at each other and restart the whole disgusting process.

Hun Su? Really? *Really?!* They weren't from the same planet.

*Blargh.*

I looked back at my sketchbook and filled in my doodle of a puppy. I guess I got it—Hun Su, with her perfectly straight, glistening hair . . . Then I noticed my hand. It looked a bit sick. As in, really green. At first I thought I was going all Ninja Turtle again. But my skin was still soft when I rubbed it. No! I was turning green with envy.

I had to find a way out of here without anyone noticing. But I couldn't. Pinned between Hun Su and Derek, I was trapped. I picked up one of the oversized menus and began "studying" it intently.

"Okay, now décor," Kate said.

Shoot. That was my cue. I couldn't put down the menu—I was still green. Hopefully no one had noticed my green fingertips peeking over the sides of the menu!

"Veronica? Knock-knock!" Derek pretended to knock on the menu.

"Uh, hi! Yeah. I'm just really hungry," I said.

"You can put the menu down for two sec—Ouch!" Derek ripped his hand away.

I may have smacked it when he tried to pull down the menu. (Okay, I totally did. I didn't mean to. It was a natural reflex.)

"Ha!" I forced a laugh. "Be careful. I bite." Worst. Joke. Ever. *Fix it quick, Veronica!* "Um, I have a whole stack of sketches right there next to my notebook," I said. "Pick what you like!"

"Okay ... ," Derek said as I heard them flipping through the pages.

"Ooooh! I like this one!" Kate cooed.

"No way, this one is totally better!" Jenny said.

Yay! They liked my ideas. They really liked my ideas.

As they continued to react, they split into two camps. They couldn't agree, and it was getting heated. How cool. My jealousy faded as the compliments kicked in. My skin was now more celery than kale.

"Stop it! Let's pick Kate's favorite!" Derek shouted over the din.

"Nooooo!" Hun Su complained.

"Ugh! Stop it, guys." Jenny instantly silenced the rabble. Queen Bee speaks. "Just, like, mix the ideas. We can mix the ideas, right?"

More silence.

Oh no. She was talking to me. "Yeah! Yeah, sure. I'm sure I can combine them," I said from behind the menu, but really I had no idea.

"Cool," Jenny said. "Everyone done being children now?"

There were embarrassed murmurs of agreement among the troops.

She let out a deep sigh. "Okay, let's talk about how I am not dealing with food this year. At all. It is way too stressful, and you all know Hun Su has issues with guacamole."

Kate started talking about possible snack options and educated us on all the food sensitivities that were popular that year. Since the controversial Peanut Ban a few years ago, their options had been a little limited. Do they go vegan? Gluten-free? Do they need to worry about everything being kosher? In the end, cupcake flavors were decided upon (red velvet and carrot cake), and everyone was blissfully happy about a job well done.

More important, I looked at my hands—the green had passed, and I could *finally* put down the menu. I realized I hadn't ordered anything, but no one seemed to care.

These were *my* people. *My new people* who talked about new things like reality TV shows and some new pop princess and her ancient actor boyfriend I had never heard of. For a second, I felt my attention wane. My brain seemed to have an urge to inform me that all this talk, this "important" talk, was not important at all. I shut it down with a *big* swig of coffee. Which, I discovered, I forgot to put sugar in. Yuck.

In the midst of my sour face, I caught a glimpse of Blake leaving. I waited, but he didn't look back over his shoulder or anything.

I tried to brush it off as no big deal. Sure, we hadn't really seen each other in almost a year (I didn't count the statue incident at the botanical garden), and last time we did I thought he was going to kiss me. Boy, was I wrong.

"Veronica, is that cool?" Kate's shrill soprano cut through my daze.

"Uh, yes!" I replied wholeheartedly to whatever she had said. For all I knew, I had just agreed to eat nothing but glass for the next five years.

Jenny smiled. "Excellent. We've never had anyone be spirited enough to take on *both* food and decorations."

My fake smile got bigger and more painful. "Both? So what will all of you be doing?" I tried to look calm.

"I don't know." Jenny thought for a moment. "Whatever, I guess."

I started organizing the sketches in front of me, finally

seeing what two themes they wanted me to combine for the dance decorations.

The first was Equestrian.

Cool, yep, got that. Saddles, hay, funky saddlebag pants. No biggie. You could mix that with anything, right?

How about vampires?

Vampires and horses. In case you missed it, that's what we're talking about, kids: vampires and horses. For our last spring formal in middle school. I opened my mouth, but nothing came out.

"We're excited to see what you can do, Vanessa. Maybe even make you a permanent member of the SFC, if the dance is a success." Derek winked at Jenny.

I wasn't sure I was supposed to see that wink. A sadness crept inside me that even the shiny newness of SFC couldn't glaze over. Here I was in my new life, but had I really changed at all? Were they just trying to use me? Good old *Vanessa*. My eyes started to tear up. *Fight it, Veronica!* I pretended to sneeze and wiped my whole face with a napkin. I refused to let myself cry.

"*Ahhhh!*" Kate cried.

Suddenly, water was pouring on us!

"Sprinklers! Run!" squealed Derek.

With that, the SFC gathered their laptops, designer purses, and smart phones and disappeared. Café Blasé was completely empty. Except for me. I didn't move. I had already looked up and knew there wasn't a sprinkler malfunction. There was a girl malfunction that had manifested as a giant rain cloud directly above my head.

The downpour lasted my entire walk home, contained to a three-foot perimeter around me. I wanted to go inside, but I was in a bit of a pickle. My desire to be horribly depressed in private was impossible without taking the storm with me. The last thing I wanted to do was spend the night sobbing and mopping, trying to clean up all the water before Dad got back from working at the club.

I sat on the front steps and let the rain do its thing. At least my sadness could clean the porch.

All I could really think about was how Charlie and I had failed to fix me. I stretched out and onto my back, thinking it would force the cloud to change position, maybe even throw it off completely, but the cloud stayed put— and I got a face full of water.

I leaped up, engulfed with anger.

I glared at the cloud as my vision turned red. My throat

burned. I knew this feeling—it was the same one I'd had when Besty blocked me from entering the art contest. I opened my mouth, sending a bolt of fire into the cloud, drying it up instantly.

I smiled. "Take that, you jerk!"

Turning to finally go inside, I spotted a large envelope leaning against the front door. I wasn't expecting anything, so it was a lovely surprise to see my name on it, typed with what looked like a typewriter. No return address. This was either from someone really cool or someone really old. Possibly both.

I looked into the settling darkness. I felt like someone was watching me, but I couldn't be sure. If there was anything I had learned in the past few days, it was that my senses weren't very sensible. Time to go inside. Shower. Tea. Then envelope.

Three hours and six minutes later:

Yeah, admittedly, that was a stupid idea.

The envelope was less of an everyday message and more of a life-altering-confusing-rip-out-your-hair-mind-blowing puzzle. Inside it, I found a newspaper article. It was about a "freak" ice storm that had encapsulated my house twelve years ago. There it was, our little bungalow with its stained-glass windows, completely frozen. Giant icicles hung from the drainpipes, like they do midwinter when Dad constantly reminds me how often "those pointy suckers kill people." So it seemed normal, until you looked at the scene surrounding my house. People were wearing shorts and sunglasses. Kids were buying ice cream from a nearby truck. I looked at the date again—July? I guess that was the "freak" part of the storm, huh?

I was only about six months old in July, which meant my mom was still around. It was bananas to think that we were in that house at the moment the picture was taken, all three of us together. I couldn't remember what that was like at all.

Sitting at the kitchen table, I flipped the article over again, examining it for any clue as to where it came from. My Calming Chamomile tea had gone cold, but I didn't care. Apparently, my house was the only one in the whole town hit by this random storm. Why hadn't Dad ever told me about it? And why would someone send this article to me? Looking around at the trail of wet footprints I'd left after the rain-cloud incident, it seemed rather obvious—it had something to do with my stupidpowers. Were they active way back then, when I was a baby? Had someone figured it out? I realized the more important question was: *Who* sent this?

I knew where to start, and he was pulling into the driveway right then.

# CHAPTER NINE
## TECHNICAL DIFFICULTIES

"You really should be in bed," Dad said with a yawn as he cracked open a beer.

"Agreed. *But*, what the hell-liocentric worldview is this and why would anyone send it to me and who would that person be?" I handed him the envelope and article.

Dad turned the envelope toward the light. "This was on the porch?"

"Yeah."

"Interesting," he said calmly.

"That's it? That's all you got?"

He returned the newspaper article to the envelope before putting it in his back pocket.

"Look, that was a really weird thing that happened years and years ago," he said.

I waited for him to continue.

Spoiler alert: He didn't.

"And?"

"And," he paused, "and there were a few people who really latched onto it. You know, conspiracy theorists. Wanted to annoy us all the time."

"Like who?"

"Just people who want to make big deals outta nothin'." He shrugged.

This made absolutely no sense. My dad. Dad. This man who wanted to know every single little detail of my day *every* day. This man who made safety his job didn't know who these "conspiracy theorists" were?

He frowned at my befuddled look. "What?"

"So, I shouldn't be concerned about this? Like, a crazy person sending me an old clipping isn't something I should worry about?"

He shifted in his chair. "It doesn't mean they're crazy. Or dangerous. Just means they want to start this garbage up all over again. Don't feed the fire, Veri. Nothing is wrong."

Was he right? He was Mr. Safety, after all. And there

were certainly more than enough things I was *already* worried about. I relaxed.

Then he opened his mouth again. "So, has anyone approached you?"

Great. "You mean, like someone with a hacksaw and bloodshot eyes?" I asked.

"Veronica," he said, and groaned.

"Daaaaad," I said with a groan right back at him. "Do you know who sent this? It really sounds like you do."

"I don't," he answered way too quickly.

"Was it She-Who-Must-Not-Be-Named?" I asked.

"Why would your mom send this to you?"

"Why are you answering questions with questions?!" I poked his arm. "And why are you being so mysterious?"

"I'm not. *You* are being dramatic."

That was the most ridiculous, stupid, repugnant, irrational thing I had ever heard. (And, no, I don't actually know what "repugnant" means, but it sounds appropriately foul.)

"Listen," he said as he took my hand in his, "I know that if anything weird or scary happened that you would tell me. Just like you told me about this, right?"

Oh, geez. He was guilt-tripping me and didn't even know it. "Right."

"We're all we got, so let's take care of each other. Which means telling each other the truth and not worrying about strange mail."

I nodded in agreement while guilt gnawed at my heart. It was true; my dad was all I had, and I was all he had. That was the biggest reason to keep my powers a secret. (Other than eternal humiliation, I mean.) If anyone found out, who knew what would happen to our little family?

Dad smooched me on the head as he headed to the living room. "You're so much like me it's ridiculous. Also, a bit annoying."

"Oh, shush, you giant booger."

"Love you, kiddo!" He clicked on the TV.

Well, freaking wonderful. That conversation left me even more confused. Could Dad have possibly seen my stupidpowers? Nah, that wasn't like him. If he had seen anything, he would have said something, right?

*Yep, Veronica, he would have said something. Just like you did when you got your powers.*

The next day I was eager to tell Charlie about the newest mystery in my life, so I invited him over.

"Who do you think sent it?" Charlie asked after I'd laid it all out.

"My dad thinks it's a conspiracy nut, and maybe it is . . . but maybe it's her." I felt my cheeks warm up.

"Do you even know where your mom is?" Charlie asked.

I shook my head. "But what if it *is* her, Charlie? What if she has these powers, too, and she's trying to reach out? I mean, it makes sense, right? Maybe that's why she went away."

"Whoa," Charlie chuckled, "that would be rad, but why wouldn't she just stop by for tea or something? You two could boil the water with your powers."

"I don't know, but—" I stopped short as I scanned the search results for the article. No matter what we typed in, we couldn't find any record of that ice storm, let alone the article about it.

"It's like it was wiped out of our town history," Charlie said. "Are you sure it happened?"

"Yeah, even Dad says it did. I don't understand why something this big wouldn't be anywhere on the Internet when I can easily find a detailed analysis of every episode of *The Golden Girls*!"

"Conspiracy!" Charlie thrust his arms in the air like he had just made a goal.

I wondered if he was right.

I spent the weekend getting ideas together for the SFC. The dance was less than two weeks away. It was time to push into high gear. Charlie stuck around and helped, despite not being the happiest camper about my new role with the SFC, and I was grateful. At least he agreed that their combination vampire-horses theme was problematic. Unfortunately, on Monday he had a much bigger problem waiting for me before lunch.

"Slow down, Charlie!" I said as I tried to understand the garble coming out of his mouth. He was talking a million miles an hour, but in a whisper.

"I—I was just in the library napping. Betsy was there, too. She was uploading her photos there since the art room is a smoking ruin. She walked away while they were transferring and I—I saw you!" he huffed and puffed.

"Betsy had a picture of me?" I said as I grabbed my sparkly blue lunch bag from my locker. "Whoop-de-doo. She's the class photographer."

He looked over his shoulder, darting suspicious glances at everyone before leaning in closer to me. "You. Were. Green."

Wait, what? "We gotta delete those pictures, Charlie. Like. Now!" I was already dashing down the hall.

I peeked through the library window. Inside, Betsy was hunched over a computer with an angry look on her face—but it was hard to tell if that look was just her normal, everyday anger.

"What do we do?" Charlie whispered as he peered over my shoulder.

"I guess we have to distract her. Then delete the pictures. Then run for our lives before she rips our spleens out through our noses."

"That sounds about right," Charlie said.

Getting Betsy to move would be easy. Although I mean "easy" as in "putting one of us in the line of great physical (and probably emotional) harm." There was only one other problem.

"If I get freaked out enough, my stupidpowers are going to do something," I reminded Charlie.

"True. We don't need her to have any more photographic evidence." Charlie thought for a second. "I guess that means I'm the bait and you're the switch!"

"But we are just deleting. Not switching anything for anything else," I told him.

Charlie nodded. "Yes, yes. You get the drift, though. You don't have to be so literal all the time."

"Literally?"

"Look alive, Betsy is coming!" Charlie dragged me around the corner and out of sight just as Betsy opened the door.

"Can you keep her away for a few minutes?" I whispered.

"I don't really have a choice, do I?" Charlie asked.

"Sorry," I said. "But you are the best ever and I totally appreciate it."

"Just try to not burn the place down." He winked at me, then chased after Betsy.

"Yo, Betsy!" he shouted as I slipped into the library.

Betsy had left the photo browser up, and it didn't take long to find the pictures of my stupidpower moment at the café. I thought I had done such a good job hiding behind that menu, but I didn't even think about the giant window behind us. Betsy had gone outside and easily caught several pics of me while I was trying to dodge glances from the SFC. I actually looked pretty good in those pictures! My hair was even normal looking. These may have been the best pictures ever taken of me. Except, you know, the green skin.

I tagged all the pictures and hit the Trash icon, and even remembered to empty the trash afterward. A hard-learned lesson from the time I had used my webcam to take some glamour shots that were so embarrassing I immediately deleted them. Or so I thought, until Dad found them and posted them on my bathroom mirror.

Anyway, these less-than-glamour shots were now deleted. But I needed to get them off the camera, too. How did I do that? This camera was *way* fancier than anything I had ever used. So many buttons! That's why the pictures were so clear and (*sigh*) undeniably of me.

It felt like too much time had passed. Charlie was great at distraction, but not that great.

Yep. I heard Charlie shout, "Hold up, Betsy! I still have to tell you something else!"

Followed by, "Don't touch me, you freak!"

I flipped through screen after screen of green me, but

there were too many to delete them one at a time. I needed them gone, now! I didn't know what else to do—

"Sorry, pretty camera." I flinched as I smashed it to the ground. The lens cap broke off, taking some of the actual lens with it. The back took a bruising, too—a big crack that destroyed the touch screen. I pressed the Power button, but nothing happened. I tried one more time for safety's sake, and still nothing. I had officially killed the evidence, and in a few seconds, Betsy would kill me, too.

Very literally.

I set the camera on the ground and artfully arranged its mangled pieces. There. It just fell. It really just fell and broke. Gravity, man. What a jerk. Yep. Yep, yep, yep. It was time to get out of here.

"What are you doing, McGowan?" Betsy yelled as she thundered into the library.

I stood and held my hands up in the universal "It wasn't me!" position. "I, uh, I think your camera fell, Betsy. I'm sorry."

"Fell?" She scrambled to pick up the pieces and cradled them like a baby. In an instant her eyes flickered from murder to sorrow and back to murder. "You did this."

"What? Me? Nooooo." I backed away from her.

Charlie stuck his head in the room and saw Betsy's rage. "Uh-oh. I think we need an adult." He looked down the hall. "Oh, crud. Ms. Watson is coming! Any adult but that one! Veri, we need to jam. Now."

"I saw you," Betsy screamed as she grabbed my arm. "I saw! And you don't want anyone to know!"

"Ow! I don't know what you're talking about." I grimaced as her thick fingers cut off my circulation.

"You're a liar!" Betsy was absolutely irate. (And, admittedly, right.)

"What is going on in here?" Ms. Watson called from the doorway. She held the top loop of Charlie's backpack—with Charlie in it—so he couldn't get away. "Unhand her! This instant!"

"She smashed my camera, Ms. Watson!" Betsy showed her the wreckage.

"The *school's* camera," Ms. Watson corrected.

"No, she bloody well didn't!" Charlie sounded really convincing, maybe because he thought he was right. He had been outside the room when I'd sent the camera to the sweet photogenic hereafter.

"Yes, she *did*. I know it!" Betsy was really starting to lose it. "She wanted to get rid of the evidence!"

She finally let me go, pushing me toward Ms. Watson and Charlie.

Ms. Watson raised an eyebrow. "The 'evidence'?"

"She. Was. Green," Betsy declared.

"Green?" Ms. Watson looked at me.

I didn't know what to do. I kept my mouth shut and rubbed my throbbing arm. I could feel something starting to happen in me. This would be the absolute worst time for a power to show up! I held my breath and tried to think of other, random things: Einstein, summer vacation, penguins in sweaters, waffles. It seemed to help!

"Charlie! Veronica!" Ms. Watson motioned for us to follow her. It was time to leave, and I knew exactly where we were going: straight to Principal Chomers and a million miles from Est-hood.

# CHAPTER TEN
## SSSSPEAKING OF PROBLEMSSSS

Ms. Watson had decided to make us sweat it out in her office.

"Shall we poke around?" Charlie asked, lifting a paper off her desk.

"No!" I smacked his hand. "Aren't we in enough trouble already?"

"Everything is going to be fine, Veri."

"Nuh-uh," I said. "I can't be found out now! I'm so close to becoming an Est. This dance means everything."

"Wait, wait, wait," Charlie said. "The dance? *That's* what you're most worried about? Not your magical superpowers?"

"They can wait until *after* the dance," I said as calmly as I could.

"No. The dance can wait! Est junk can wait!" he said. "This is getting serious, Veri."

"*You* are talking about serious?" I was astounded. "You're the one who thinks this whole mess is awesome. I'm going through with the dance, Charles. My stupidpowers aren't going to stop me."

"Unbelievable," Charlie muttered.

"What are we talking about in here?" Ms. Watson said. Charlie and I jumped.

"Nothing," I said flatly. "Nothing at all."

"Mr. Weathers, Ms. McGowan. What are we to do with you?" Ms. Watson asked as she got into her chair.

"Let us go home, perhaps?" Charlie said.

I lowered my head.

Ms. Watson didn't even crack a smile. "What happened? And why do I have Betsy swearing that you were green and you destroyed her camera, Ms. McGowan?"

"Well," I sputtered, "I *was* green . . ."

Charlie's eyes nearly popped out of his head.

". . . with envy," I added. "Isn't that how the saying

goes? And I think it was just really apparent from my expression when Betsy photographed me."

Charlie caught on quickly. "Yes! And we went to Betsy to ask her not to use those unflattering pictures of Veronica."

"B-but by the time we were all together, the camera was already on the ground," I said. Now that I was fibbing, I sensed a stupidpower flaring up. I felt sneaky and slimy, like a snake.

"If it was an accident, why would Betsy blame you for breaking the camera?" Ms. Watson asked.

"Because Betsy *hatessssss* me," I actually hissed. I snapped my mouth closed and looked at Charlie, mentally telling him to take over.

"Uh, yes," Charlie picked up where I left off. "Betsy bullies Veronica on a regular basis. Everyone in school knows that. Hates her guts, some would say."

I nodded in silent agreement.

"And what was the scenario in which you 'turned green'?" Ms. Watson added air quotes to her question.

I was scared to open my mouth. I needed to mind my s's.

"I wa—I mean, at Bla—I mean, at . . . the café with . . . the formal club, when I got—" Crud. What was an s-less word for *envious*?

Luckily, Ms. Watson interpreted my awkwardness as embarrassment.

"So, you saw the Spring Formal Club? And you were jealous of them?" she asked.

"No. I'm *on* the S-SFC." I managed a stutter instead of a hiss. The stupidpower was fading as long as I was telling the truth. "I, uh, wasn't jealous of them, I guess."

"What were you jealous of?" Ms. Watson asked in a voice that was oddly soothing.

I could feel Charlie staring at me. Wasn't this humiliating enough? Now I had to fess up to something that would make Charlie tease me for the next bazillion years?

"It wasn't anything, really. There was just someone else there. Can we please not talk about this?" I muttered to the floor.

Charlie let out an exasperated sigh. "Blake," he answered for me.

"You don't understand."

"*I* don't understand?" Charlie looked hurt. "Pretty sure I'm the *only* one who understands."

Ms. Watson furrowed her brow. "Agreed. I definitely don't understand what either of you are talking about. What I do understand is that we have damaged property and three preteens who can't seem to get along."

"It's not Charlie's fault," I said. "Principal Chomers should let him go."

"We are both in this," Charlie said, more to Ms. Watson than me.

Ms. Watson nodded. "Well, then you should both be pleased. After this discussion, I have chosen *not* to take this up with Principal Chomers."

"Oh, thank heavens," Charlie said. "Is there anything I can do for you? Do you need a kidney? I have a spare."

"*But,*" Ms. Watson continued, ignoring Charlie, "you'll be spending the next two afternoons with me. After school."

(I half expected her to belt out a super-villainous "Bwah-ha-ha!")

"Detention?" I asked.

"Yes." She stared at me, her eyes narrowed. "That's what they call it."

"Elementary, my dear Watson." Charlie tipped an imaginary hat and puffed on an equally imaginary pipe. "But you seem to have missed a very important clue. We didn't do anything wrong."

"I don't know who did what, but I get the feeling that no one is telling me the truth . . . on more than one account."

I had a question. "So, what about Betsy? Isn't she in trouble, too?"

"She physically accosted you, Veronica. There will be a punishment, certainly, but I'll deal with her separately. Although actually, it might be therapeutic for the three of you to serve your sentence together, now that I think about it." She nodded, agreeing wholeheartedly with herself. "Maybe you can work things out. Ensure that we never again have a situation like the one we saw today."

"But—" I sputtered.

"See you back here at three."

And that was all she wrote. Well, I mean, all she said.

"Thank you, Ms. Watson," I said as Charlie and I gathered up our things.

I pulled the door shut behind us.

"What was up with you in there?" Charlie asked.

"Nothing, I-I'm just tired," I lied. Truth was, I was starting to feel very alone. Charlie was doing his best to help, but this was something he couldn't really understand.

My stupidpowers could cause a lot of trouble and real damage to him. That wasn't how friendship was supposed to work.

"Hi, guys!" I called as I set my backpack down on the bleachers. Being outside for non-gym activities was a treat reserved for the coolest of clubs.

Kate looked up from a thick history book. "Hi, Veronica!"

The rest of the Ests seemed very occupied, nay, obsessed with their phones. To get their attention I knew I'd have to make a big impression, so I came prepared. In one swoop, I whipped out the gigantic binder I had painstakingly put together over the weekend. It held all my ideas for the dance. And there were . . . a lot. And maybe some glitter glue. Or maybe all the glitter glue I owned.

They were going to freaking lose their beautiful minds when they saw all the work I'd done!

"So, here are my thoughts for decorations." I grandly opened the binder to reveal its super-glam interior. There they were, the horses and the vampires and the vampire horses!

"This is, like, really amazing," Derek said in disbelief.

My heart soared as the other Ests—except Jenny, who remained entranced by her phone—nodded in agreement. My happiness was at an all-time high, which instantly made me worry. This would be the exact time that stupidpowers would come out. Happy! Happy? What stupidpowers come from happy? I could feel my toe start to tap, and I wasn't making it tap. That's when I noticed that my head was bobbing as if there was some really great music playing. News flash: there wasn't.

I was dancing. Oh my gawd, I was dancing. Uncontrollably. The stupidest of stupidpowers had me moonwalking in front of the SFC.

*Stop, Veronica, STOP!* I needed to gain control of my limbs. The entire SFC was staring at me.

"Ha!" I pretended to laugh as I busted into some snazzy jazz hands. "These are just examples of dances no one should *ever* do at a dance!"

"Go, Veronica! Go, Veronica!" Titan Williams (Funniest) shouted.

The SFC all smiled and laughed as they clapped a beat for me to dance to—except for Jenny, who was still phone obsessed.

Titan joined me. His dance was definitely a joke. It was the same one my dad would bust out occasionally at a wedding. I think it was called the Running Man? Anyway, Titan hammed it up for a few minutes while my stupidpowers kept me dancing. In fact, after he did his final hip thrust, I was still going strong, feeling happy and like I was finally part of the group. That happiness was a problem, because it meant my powers would keep me dancing indefinitely. It was getting awkward again.

I worked up all my will and pushed down my happy feelings. I pushed 'em down as hard as I possibly could. It felt uncomfortable, like holding my breath, or pulling on a too-tight pair of jeans fresh out of the dryer, but I seemed to be reapproaching normalcy. My arms and legs slowed down, and I had control over them again. It worked! I actually controlled my powers! But I'd had to hide my feelings to do it. If I became Artiest, would I have to constantly keep squashing my own emotions?

"I know all of you are having fun, or something, but listen up!" Jenny crowed, waving her phone. "Dark Rooms announced they are playing a surprise show Friday at the Oil City Thunderdome! We *have* to get tickets."

"It's impossible, man," Titan said, sighing. "I already heard it sold out in seconds."

What I was about to say would definitely change things, but what was really strange was that, for about fifteen seconds, I hesitated to even say it. I knew this would raise me way up in the eyes of the Ests, but something about it felt icky. Despite that icky feeling, I said it anyway. "*Uhh*, guys? What if I could get you into an even more secret, smaller show that Dark Rooms is doing? For free?"

In unison, their jaws dropped.

"What did you say?" Hun Su asked.

"I, um, well, I know their drummer. You see, my dad and his mom are cousins, so he's my second cousin or something? I don't know, really, but sometimes we have Thanksgiving together . . . Anyway, uh, they are playing a secret show under a different name at Count's on Wednesday."

"*Pfft*," Jenny said. "That's a twenty-one-and-over club. Even if you are telling the truth, we couldn't get in."

I smiled, despite wanting to crush Jenny in my hands. And again, I hesitated.

"Maybe we could come to Thanksgiving?" Titan joked.

Everyone laughed.

"That's pretty neat, though, Veronica," Kate added, though I noticed Jenny shot her a look. Kate immediately looked away from me and back to her book.

"Well," I said, "my dad is the bouncer there. I can find a way to get us in."

Aaaaaand they were back.

"OMG! Really, Val?" Derek put his arm around me.

"It's still Veronica, actually. And yeah, we can go, if it's only a few of us."

Hun Su lost it as she and Derek jumped up and down.

"You're one hundred percent sure?" Jenny pressed.

"One hundred percent sure." I cheered and flung my hands up—as one does when one is lying through her teeth.

# CHAPTER ELEVEN
## (NOT SO) SOLITARY CONFINEMENT

There it was: three o'clock. Our usual time of joy and freedom was now a slow trudge of doom to the library for detention.

"Oh, one of my favorite napping spots in the entire school," Charlie squealed.

"You have more than one?" I asked.

"But of course," Charlie said, "and I rank them by quietness, comfortableness, and proximity to a vending machine."

"Where does the library rank?" I asked as we walked up the stairs.

"Third," he continued, "out of thirty-two."

Outside the library, Charlie flung up his hood as he

used his body weight to push the door open. "Snoozeroo City, here I come."

But the library did not look like Snoozeroo City or *any* relaxing suburb from Charlie's imagination. Ms. Watson was waiting there and had turned all but four of the chairs up onto the tables, just like the janitorial staff did. In one of the chairs, a steely-eyed Betsy already sat.

"Come in," Ms. Watson barked. "Sit."

Charlie and I sat down next to each other, with Charlie across from Betsy.

"Now," Ms. Watson began, sitting next to Betsy, "here is how life goes: You *children* may never get along, but you have to learn to be in the same room together and not cause a scene. A little respect, a little understanding—that is a basic requirement in life. And that is what we will be doing for the next two afternoons: being in the same room. Without causing a scene. Sure, Betsy might think it's ridiculous how loosey-goosey Veronica is. And maybe Betsy thinks Charlie's accent is dumb and made up."

"It is," Betsy said.

"Maybe we should all sit quietly?" Charlie suggested, and for once he, Betsy, and I agreed on something.

Ms. Watson took a seat behind the main library desk

and proceeded to mostly ignore us. She had given the impression that our detention was akin to some kind of water torture, sure to break all of us in the end. She was right. Just sitting at the table, we were soon bored out of our skulls.

"I never thought I'd say this," Charlie asked, "but can we do some work or something? You know, library research?"

Ms. Watson looked over and, after considering, nodded.

Soon, Charlie and I were wandering the aisles, secretly trying to find anything that might help us learn about the mystery article I'd been sent. But I came up empty-handed.

"Nothing here, either," he said, standing in front of the cookbook section. "I looked *really* hard."

"You can't just make a newspaper vanish into thin air," I whispered.

"The microfiche machine," Betsy's voice grumbled from back by the chairs. "Prolly some pictures and junk there."

The microfiche reader! I hadn't even thought of that old, dusty contraption.

"I'm so confused," Charlie said. "Did Betsy just help us?"

"I think she did?" I wasn't sure. "Let's just enjoy this moment."

Fifteen minutes later, I was still trying to get the dang machine to work with zero luck whatsoever. It simply wouldn't power on.

"It's useless, Veri," Charlie finally said.

My frustration had mounted to a dangerous level. I stared at the faulty plug—and a massive static shock of stupidpowers shot out of my fingers and into the machine.

Whoa.

I flipped the On switch for the microfiche reader— and it came alive, a bright light shining behind the screen. I was really proud of myself. The first successful result of my superpowers. I kicked the power cord out of sight. Hopefully no one noticed that the machine wasn't even plugged in.

Once we figured out how to find the film we needed, we finally found the same article that was sent to me. Encouraged, we started scanning newspapers from the next few days and weeks.

Charlie leaned in to get a better look at the screen. "Whoa, Veri, look at this."

He pointed at an article about another rare storm,

about sixty miles north. That storm hit almost a week after ours. The article also referred to yet another strange and powerful storm that had happened a few days before that in a nearby town.

"Add another check mark to the Government Cover-Up Conspiracy!" Charlie said excitedly.

Another fifteen minutes of looking resulted in many more unusual storms, including one with reported "burning winds," in even more surrounding towns.

"We need to map these," I told Charlie.

"That's a good idea. See if there is a trail."

Just as it was getting really interesting, Ms. Watson called time on detention. The janitor was waiting to lock up the library.

More sleuthing would have to wait until the next day. I had to prepare for another event I had planned the next morning: convincing a very large man that a few small preteens wouldn't cause any trouble.

Occasionally there is a night where Dad leaves for work at the club before I'm home from school and he doesn't get back until I'm asleep. On those days, the following morning we go out to breakfast before school. Usually it's pretty fun. This morning, not so much.

"You're outta your noodle, Veronica." Dad chuckled as he shook his head. "Letting Charlie in every once in a while is one thing—a thing I probably shouldn't be doing in the first place, mind you—but letting in a bunch of your new friends? Nuh-uh. Sorry."

He crammed half a cheese Danish in his mouth and took a big swig of coffee before he went back to pretending to read an article about ear candling in *Yoga Today*.

Our Parkin's Family Diner waiter refilled Dad's mug, noticed the uncomfortable silence as I glared at my dad, and cheerfully said, "I'll check on you two in a minute."

I knew there was no way Dad would ever okay the Ests coming to the club—at least, not right off the bat. He would take some major convincing, but I was willing to do the hard work to become an Est.

I sipped my juice, never averting my gaze. I knew he could feel me watching; his feigned interest in yoga could only hold out for so long.

I could wait.

I had a lot of patience.

As long as this was all resolved by nine p.m. tomorrow.

Finally he tossed the magazine back onto the pile on the windowsill and met my stare. "This isn't open for debate," he said. "Those kids get caught, I lose my job, probably *both* jobs, then we lose our house, and we starve to death in the cold. No more delicious fresh Danishes or choco-banana-peanut-butter waffles for us."

I didn't think it would be *this* hard. There weren't many topics that weren't open for debate in our house, aside from which Beatle is the best Beatle. (Don't listen to my dad, it's totally John.)

"No one will even notice them," I said. "It'll be like they aren't even there, I swear. Besides, it can't be *that* big of a deal."

Dad raised his eyebrows. "You realize that letting them in would be breaking the law, right?"

"But you let Charlie in." Dad's reasoning on this was stupid. Stupid, I say. (Just not out loud.)

Dad leaned in and lowered his voice. "I let Charlie in because he is *one* person. A person we trust; not some random kids you barely know. Trust is everything."

"I know, I know," I mumbled. Trust, trust, blah, blah, blah. "But just this once—"

"Zip it. I'm not saying it again." He gave me the look that said he really, really meant it.

"*Gah!* I'm *so* close to being an Est! You treat me like a baby!"

With that, Dad got up and headed toward the door.

"Dad!" I cried after him.

"Hey, grown-up," he called back, pulling a cigar from his pocket as he stepped outside, "thanks for breakfast."

And with that, the dude left me with the bill.

With my allowance and all the change from the bottom of my purse, I managed to pay the bill and leave our waiter a seventy-eight-cent tip. I bet he loved that. Hopefully he wouldn't be our waiter next time.

The walk to school was long, and I knew Dad thought it would give me time to think, time to be reasonable and all that garbage, but what it really did was give me time to get more irritated. My dad was a rule breaker for most of his life. A big flippin' rule breaker. But never when it came to me. He was as bad as Charlie sometimes.

A buzzing sound caught my attention as I spotted a couple dozen small yellowjackets starting to buzz around me!

*"Ahh!"* I screamed. On closer inspection, I could see their wings each had a little skull and crossbones on them. One yellowjacket even had an eye patch. These were more stupidpower manifestations.

"Ow!" I shouted as one of them stung me. I swore I heard a little, evil laugh. Wait, were they all laughing at me? Before I knew it, I was running from the swarm! I made it about three blocks before I ran out of steam. I hid behind a tree, covering my face with my arms.

Much to my surprise, after a few breaths, they disappeared.

By the time detention rolled around that day, I had managed to accept that Dad wasn't going to change his mind, and I would have to break the news to the Ests before they showed up at the club the next night. I was not looking forward to that. Even less than I was looking forward to being stuck in the library.

"Here we are again," sighed Ms. Watson. She looked gloomy—nowhere near as crisp or stern as usual—as she sat behind the librarian's desk. A fresh issue of a tabloid magazine was open in front of her.

"What did we learn yesterday?" she asked as she

turned a page in the magazine. "Respect? Is respect even real?"

Charlie and I shared a look. Ms. Watson apparently had a bad day.

"You can try and try and try," Ms. Watson continued, "but it doesn't mean that anyone will take your efforts seriously. Or back you up and work for justice. Some people want the status quo over truth!" She looked at us like we knew what she was talking about and should also be outraged.

"Are, uh, you okay, Ms. Watson?" Charlie asked.

"I am fine," she replied quickly. "I just lost my job."

"Then why are you here?" Charlie said, deeply puzzled.

Ms. Watson put her hand on her forehead. "No, no. I apologize. I don't mean this job. I mean my . . . other job."

"Where else do you work?" I asked.

"It's nothing," she said.

"Okay," I said sheepishly.

"Just don't ever give up everything for your job is what I'm saying."

Charlie leaned over and whispered to me, "She's gone off her rocker."

The *chut-chut* of an automatic camera shutter made Ms. Watson wince. "Enjoying the new camera, Betsy?" she asked uncertainly.

Sure enough, Betsy had a camera, but I wouldn't call it new. It was huge and held together by duct tape. The lens cover dangled by a twist tie.

Betsy grunted an acknowledgment.

"Good," Ms. Watson said. "May I speak with you in private?"

Charlie and I used their little meet-up as an excuse to get back to our research. On one of the tables nestled way back by the encyclopedias we stretched out a state map and marked every place there had been a freak storm or other weird incident. It was pretty wild—they formed a trail that followed right along the highway for about one hundred miles north. The last storm had been in a tiny town I had heard of, but never been to, called Westchester.

"Why did they stop there?" Charlie wondered.

"Well, if my mom also has these powers, maybe that's where she went. Maybe that's where she is now."

Charlie shrugged.

There was only one way to find out if my suspicions were true, but that would cause some major issues with my dad. Charlie and I put the map away and went to rejoin Betsy and Ms. Watson to wait out the last hour of our detention. But we discovered Betsy was leaving with an elderly woman in a faded plaid dress and a crumpled felt hat.

"What the heck?" Charlie asked Ms. Watson. "Why does she get to go early?"

Ms. Watson sighed. "Betsy is leaving for an appointment at the request of her legal guardian."

Legal guardian? I recognized the woman; it was Betsy's grandmother. She had gotten her dentures from my dad. I'd heard Betsy's parents had split up last summer, but I didn't know she'd been sent to live with her grandma. Suddenly Betsy's transition from Est to Goth chick made more sense. For once I actually felt bad for her.

"What does it matter?" Ms. Watson said after they left. "You two are also dismissed."

"Woo-hoo!" Charlie threw his backpack on and did a little dance of happiness to pass the time while I got my stuff together.

Before going, I stopped at Ms. Watson's desk. She was mindlessly drawing mustaches and monocles on celebrities in her tabloid magazine.

"That's a great look for Sandra Bullock," I offered.

"What? Oh, yeah. Well enjoy your evening, Ms. McGowan."

"Ms. Watson," I asked, "did you give Betsy that camera?"

She nodded. "Affirmative."

"That was nice of you."

She furrowed her brow. "I just saw a situation that needed to be rectified. 'Nice' has nothing to do with it."

"Well, I'm sure your help made a big difference to Betsy."

"Really?" She sounded amazed.

"Yeah. We have a lot of problems. I think most of us need someone to 'rectify' things."

She paused and stared at me like this was the first time she had ever thought about it.

"That's why you became a guidance counselor, right?" I asked. "To make a difference?"

"Oh yes! Yes, indeed." The look in Ms. Watson's eye

was suddenly far away, like she was deep in thought. Then she started to slowly nod her head, like she was realizing something for the first time. "Guidance counselors can really change lives and help ignored and belittled voices be heard." Her eyes sparkled. "Young voices, I mean. Not adult ones."

"Veri!" Charlie called from the door.

"Coming!" I smiled at Ms. Watson, who, much to my surprise, smiled back.

On the way home, I wanted to see the art contest, which had just gone up in the gym. Charlie was done with school, though, so he split. I quickly spotted Betsy's *two* entries and felt my newfound empathy for her melting away. One was a photograph of an abandoned shoe in an intersection and the other was a drawing of the same picture. They were really good, but don't tell anyone I said that. Believe me, Betsy already knew.

"Where's your stuff?"

I turned to see Blake.

"Hi, uh, what are you doing here?" I managed to spit out.

"Just meeting some people at the football field when they're done with practice," he answered.

"They still let you in here? Once I'm in high school, I'm never coming back." I was quite proud of myself for actually making a joke.

"I know, right?" He laughed. "So? Art?"

"Oh! Well, I don't have anything in the contest this year."

"That's a bummer. Art is your thing, right?"

"Yeah, I was just too late entering."

He nodded as if this was something that happened to him every single day of his life.

I didn't know what to say, so there was an awkward silence.

"We'll see you tomorrow?" he asked. "Jenny told me about the show. Really cool."

*You mean the show that I need to tell everyone they can't go to?*

"You're coming?" I croaked.

"If that's all right."

"Yeah, of course!" I gushed. "See you tomorrow night."

"Rad." He left, waving over his shoulder.

Well, there ya had it. My dad had left me no other option: I had to totally disobey him.

# CHAPTER TWELVE
## MISSION: INCOMPREHENSIBLE

Getting Derek, Hun Su, Jenny, Titan, and Blake into the club wouldn't be too hard if I timed everything exactly, completely, without fail, 100 percent perfectly with no one noticing me. I could do that, right? It wasn't like I had some weird condition that made me randomly have very noticeable outbursts.

Ha-ha.

The plan was fairly simple. All I had to do was get them through the club's broken side door and sneak them up the stairs into a corner spot near the rafters. No one would ever know. As long as no one ever saw us.

That was plan A. I didn't have a plan B, but I soon

learned B stands for "You would B stupid not to have a plan B."

Derek and Titan arrived at our meeting spot (around the back corner of the club) about fifteen minutes late. I had spent that fifteen minutes biting my nails and holding in about a year's worth of anxiety. So far, no stupidpowers had appeared, which was a relief. A painful, need-to-be-constantly-vigilant-and-not-show-your-feelings relief, but a relief nonetheless.

"You guys know where Hun Su is? Or Jenny?"

"Yeah, they're on their way," Derek said after checking his texts. "Jenny loves to make people wait."

"Hey, B-man!" Titan hollered over my shoulder.

*"Shh!"* My dad was just around the corner at the front door. Wait, did he say "B-man"? I turned to see Blake coming toward us. He was wearing ripped jeans and a super old, threadbare Mickey Mouse T-shirt. Really, I couldn't think of anyone else who could pull that off.

"OMG! Blake!" Hun Su exclaimed behind me in a voice one would normally save for winning the lottery.

I turned to see that Hun Su was wearing an adorable Minnie Mouse T-shirt. Ooof.

Did I mention it was tight? Like, really tight? I looked

down at my own purple shirt with its crocheted hem. And saw my sneakers below it. Unlike the other Est girls, there was barely anything filling out my T-shirt to block the view of my feet.

Blake gave a sly chuckle. "Great minds." He turned to me. "What's the plan, McGowan?"

"We'll just need to be really quiet," I answered.

"I thought your dad was gonna let us in?" Hun Su asked.

Blake laughed. "We really don't want Veronica's dad involved in this. Trust me."

Inside, I swooned a little bit.

"Yeah," I agreed. "There's a spot where we can hang out and no one will see us. It might be a little cramped with six people, but we'll manage."

"What about Kate and her brothers?" Derek asked as he pointed to the three people walking toward us.

"Nine people including me," I whispered as I did my best not to panic. We were doomed. The spot near the rafters was too small.

Blake leaned into me. "Come on, Veronica, a little mischief never hurt anyone."

For that, I happily silenced the alarms going off in my

head and waved the others to follow me quietly. The club was full, and the opening band had already started their set. It was perfect timing. The room was dark, and this far-off corner was the last place anyone was looking. Except one dude, who regularly had to hide back here.

"Holy crap on a cracker. Veri, what is going on?" Charlie asked as I sent the Ests, Kate's brothers, and Blake up the steps to the little loft area.

"They're just gonna watch the show. No biggie," I said. Once my "guests" had made it up the stairs, I added, "Please don't tell my dad."

"I won't." Charlie crossed his heart.

Above us, the Ests had crammed onto the little landing in the loft between the rafters. They were having fun, obviously, as giggles drifted down to us.

"Not much room up there for you," Charlie noted.

"It's okay. There were a few more people than I expected. I'm just glad they made it up without getting caught."

Charlie and I sat behind a stack of chairs and listened as Dark Rooms started up. I was so nervous, it took all my concentration just to keep my stupidpowers at bay. Charlie kept looking at me. I think he could tell I was about to lose it.

"Where do you think missing socks go?" he wondered aloud, trying to distract me from my nerves. "Do you think they're stolen out of dryers by elves or something?"

"Probably," I said, trying to relax. I couldn't. I smelled cigar smoke. Dad was nearby.

"Are ya sure? I'm holding out for aliens."

I spotted my dad outside the window, just below the loft. He didn't usually smoke there! If he looked up, he would easily see all the Ests! At least the music was loud enough that he shouldn't hear them.

"Veronica?" Blake whispered. He had crawled down from the loft.

I gestured for him to follow me into the corner, away from Charlie. I leaned against a large power cord plugged into the wall to make room for both of us.

"What's up?" My voice went up about three octaves.

"I just wanted to say thanks for this from all of us. I know it probably isn't easy with your pops." He glanced up, and I did, too.

The Ests were waving their thanks at me from the rafters—well, all but one. I couldn't help but notice that Jenny wasn't joining in.

I turned to Blake to say it was no big deal, but there

was something wrong with my tongue. I swooshed it around in my mouth. Was it in a knot? A nod would have to suffice.

"Seriously. Thanks," Blake said as he touched my hand. *He touched my hand.*

I backed up against the power cord behind me, grabbing it to steady myself, as Blake kept looking at me.

I felt this intense electricity between us. It was magical. It was amazing. It was . . . It was an *actual* surge of electricity that went through my hand and into the power strip and fried the entire circuit breaker.

Instantly, the lights all went out.

*BOOM!*

There went the transformer outside. *Aaaaand* all the power for all the homes within a five-block radius.

A shrill cry filled the club. I knew exactly where it had come from: me.

They got the generators on pretty quickly. Too quickly, in fact. I only had half of my guests out the door by the time my dad, flashlight in hand, spotted them. Even worse was that all the commotion had gotten the club's owner, Mr. G, out of his office, and he had also seen the giggling teen exodus.

"Get back here!" Dad yelled after them as he ran to the door. I hadn't had time to get out and was hiding behind the chairs.

I heard Titan say, "Isn't that our dentist?" as they fled into the night.

"Stupid kids," Dad muttered as he turned toward my hiding place—and his eyes widened as he saw me.

"And what the heck do you think you're doing, missy?" he called. "Outside! Now!"

He had made me wait out there forever while he talked to his boss, which wasn't a good sign. I leaned against the brick wall of the club and prayed for a quick, painless death.

"So you're saying you weren't with them?" he scoffed when he finally came out. "And you can't tell me who they are?"

"Nope."

"This is not cool, Veronica." He pointed at me. "Don't lie."

Charlie wandered out of the broken side door and seemed to immediately regret this decision.

"Who were those kids, Charlie?" Dad asked, still looking at me.

I stared Charlie down. *Do. Not. Tell.*

Dad was getting impatient. "Someone has to tell me or Veronica is grounded. Indefinitely."

Charlie offered them up instantly. "It was Derek and Jenny and Hun Su and Titan and Blake. Oh, and Kate and her brothers!"

"That's all I needed to know," Dad growled. "Veronica, wait in the car. Go home, Charlie." Dad put out his cigar and went back inside.

"Charlie!" I screeched, smacking him on the shoulder.

"You should have given them up, Veri," he said. "I heard your dad talking to Mr. G. He wanted to fire your dad. If the cops had found them, the club would've been closed. He had to beg to keep his job."

"Why are you on his side?" I asked. Charlie was supposed to be my friend and support *me*. This wasn't what I wanted. I knew it was a crappy situation for Dad, but in the end, no one had gotten hurt. Why couldn't Charlie see that?

"I better get in the car," I said as I looked at the ground.

"Veri?" Charlie called after me as I walked away.

Once I was in the car, I was smart enough to keep my mouth shut. The fewer words I said, the less incriminating evidence there would be.

Dad broke the silence. "What's with you lately?"

Talk about broad questions.

"Nothing," I said.

"*That* was nothing? Tell me the truth."

"Dad, why did Mom go away?" I asked. If he wanted truth from me, I needed some from him. If Mom had stupidpowers and he knew it, I needed to know, too.

"You want to talk about this now?"

"Yeah." I was scared enough of what his answer might be that a chunk of my hair was turning white. I could see the whiteness slowly glide down a few strands that hung over my shoulder in my reflection in the car window. Luckily Dad couldn't see it from where he was sitting.

"We didn't agree on how to raise you," he said matter-of-factly.

That wasn't scary. The color seeped back into my hair. "But, that's pretty much like all parents, right?" I asked.

"It *is* true for most parents, but it was different with us." Dad took a deep breath before he went on. "You're not a baby anymore, so I'm going to tell you something, but it's also going to be the end of this discussion."

"But why?" My interest had been raised by about a zillion degrees.

"Just agree that you are gonna leave it alone."

I didn't want to agree, but a little info was better than none. "Okay, okay. Just tell me!"

"I didn't feel like you were safe with your mom around." He blurted it out like the words hurt his tongue.

Safe? That was really all the confirmation I needed, right? What could be less safe than randomly destroying things?

Mom had superpowers.

"But—" I started.

"Shush," Dad demanded. "I said that was all I wanted to say and that's all I'm saying right now."

"One question—" I begged.

"No."

"You can't just say something like that and then shut it

down. That's not fair! You go on and on and on about trust all the time, but you don't even trust me enough to tell me the truth?"

"That's not accurate." He used his thumb to point backward toward the club. "You're the one who is keeping secrets and acting sketchy."

Dad wasn't wrong, but I was still irritated. I just wanted answers.

He rolled his window down. I knew what that meant—he was getting hot because he was mad. "You were a jerk tonight, kid. I don't owe you anything. In fact, for this stunt, your summer is going to be spent working reception at the dental office."

We said nothing else the rest of the drive. Did Dad know *I* had stupidpowers? It didn't seem like he did, especially if he thought Mom was dangerous because of hers. Now I definitely couldn't tell him the truth.

Wouldn't he think I was dangerous, too?

# CHAPTER THIRTEEN
## IN YOUR BEDROOM NO ONE CAN HEAR YOU SCREAM

Once safely in my bedroom, I flung myself onto my bed and screamed into my pillow, but that wasn't enough for my stupidpowers. Suddenly I couldn't hear my own scream anymore. I lifted my head and let out a yell, but no noise came out of my mouth.

*Woo! Woo! Woo! Woo!* a car alarm wailed outside, interrupting my screech-fest. Then another car alarm, and another, and another. I looked out the window and saw that every single car on the entire street had its alarm going off. Whoa. A few minutes of frantic, confused activity later, and all the owners had stopped the noise and the flashing lights.

Back to it, I screamed again. I felt the air whipping through my lungs and throat, but still no audible scream.

*"Bree! Breeeee! Ooh-ooh-ooh-ooh!"* echoed from downstairs. The house alarm?

An annoyed swear word from Dad assured me that it was just the security system going awry, not burglars. "Piece o' crap," he added as he typed in the secret code with a series of beeps.

Okay, one more shot at this whole screaming thing. Bracing myself, I screamed using as much force as I could, but no sound came out. None. I kept going, trying harder and harder. Off went the car alarms again, then the house alarm joined in as the front window in my room cracked. Out of breath, I stopped my silent scream. Then I noticed Einstein, who was pawing at his ears, like he does when he hears a high-pitched whistle. Holy cow. He could hear my scream. I had gone supersonic.

"Son of a—!"

It was a noisy night, for sure. My octave-smashing range had not only tripped all the house and car alarms on the block, but it also had somehow set up a loop in our own security system that caused it to go off randomly all night. Which, in turn, made my dad go off in swearing binges all night. Super fun, guys.

By morning I was exhausted in numerous ways. Obviously, the no-sleep thing was a component, but I also felt worn-out. And weary. And some other word that means emotionally tired. If that word exists, I was too tired to think of it. The dance was less than a week away, my mom was dangerous, my dad was furious, and I was a big old mess of confused emotions.

While Charlie and I walked to school, I caught him up on my "dangerous" mom situation. I was relieved that it confused him as much as it confused me.

Then I had a thought that I knew I'd go through with, even though my gut told me it was a bad idea.

"Maybe I'll take the bus out to Westchester?" I shrugged.

"You can't do that by yourself, Veri. Actually, I'm not certain you should go at all."

"I kinda have to, though, right?"

After a moment, Charlie nodded. "I guess I would want to if I were you. But I'm coming with you."

"What about Ms. Watson? She'll be all over us if we both miss school today."

"Ugh. Good point."

"I'll go by myself. It'll be all right," I said even though I had no idea if it would.

I was off to see my mom for the first time in eleven years. She had run away. She probably had superpowers. What could possibly go wrong?

The bus ride was long, but it gave me some time to catch up on the sleep I'd missed the night before.

I had absolutely no idea what to do once I got to Westchester. I had brought one picture of my mom from the box back home. Showing it to the local barista didn't help, so I asked a bank teller, a garbage man, and a dog walker. By midafternoon, I felt out of options. No one recognized her. Either she was a hermit or she didn't actually live here. The bus would be coming back soon. This was a dumb idea from the start. I bought a soda and went to draw in the park near the bus station.

I started to sketch a woman in the park who was reading a book. She had the reddest hair I had ever seen—even redder than Charlie's—and a tired face. About three-quarters of the way through sketching, I found myself in the middle of a very familiar cowlick. I held the sketch away from my face. It couldn't be. Here in black and white, I could see her. This woman looked like an older, box-hair-dye version of my mom!

How could I be sure, though? What kind of weirdo goes up to a stranger and asks, "Hey, are you my mom?" I decided to explore a suspicion that had been lurking in my belly for quite some time. Opening my phone, I found the contact I had pilfered from Dad's phone. My fingers shook as I pressed the Call button.

Within seconds, Red was digging through her fringed handbag.

"Hello?" she said. I could see her say the word at the same time I heard it through the phone.

I said nothing, I didn't move, I just watched her.

"Who is this?" She waited a beat, then said, "Go to hell!" and hung up.

I hadn't even moved the phone from my ear yet when the feelings hit hard. Literally. My stupidpowers punched me in the gut, sending me flying backward. A shrub broke my fall, but this made me even more mad. I stood up and got ready to take another punch from my inner self.

"Just kill me now!" I yelled at the air.

"A little dramatic," a familiar voice said behind me.

Something in me still wasn't working right, so when I turned to see Betsy, my brain didn't seem to process it with the usual amount of fear.

I managed to squeak out, "What are you doing here?"

"The plan was to catch even more of your alien mutant stuff so I can ruin your life," she told me.

"Oh," I said, trying to wrap my mind around everything that had just happened.

"You didn't do anything until just now, so it was kinda a waste of time. I got much better shots of all your weirdness back home." She scrolled through pictures on her camera before she popped out its memory card and put it in her pocket. "It's all on that card, and don't you forget it," she said.

Disturbed, I looked back to see if the woman with my hair was still sitting aways off in the park. She was.

"Can you stay focused, please?" Betsy said. "I was talking to you. I'm sure finding your mom and all that was important, but not to me."

"How'd you know that was my mom?"

"You both have that stupid hair flip."

"*Hmm.*" Numbness had set in and I couldn't seem to figure out what emotion I should be having. I should have been scared because Betsy was there, but she hadn't tried to kill me yet. I should have been raging at my mom still. I should have been crying because that was probably what was expected of a girl whose long-lost mom had just told her to "go to hell," but there wasn't anything there. It was almost as if my stupidpower outburst had wiped me out.

I decided to ask Betsy something I had been wondering about. "Hey, Betsy? Can I ask you a question?"

"I think you probably will even if I say no," she said.

"So, you've seen my . . ."

"Freakishness?"

"You've seen what I can do."

"And? Wasn't there supposed to be a question in there?" she said, and sighed.

"You don't seem fazed or like you have safety concerns," I said. "You even helped us in the library, with the microfiche machine. That's how I figured out I should come here."

Betsy shrugged. "This is the most exciting thing that's ever happened in our crap hometown. It's kind of like real-life performance art," she added. "And that still wasn't a question."

For some inexplicable reason, her answer made me feel better. Could Betsy possibly not be 100 percent pure evil?

"Okay. Actual question: Do you think my mom looks like she has the same . . . issues I do?" I stared at a dandelion that was arching toward the sun.

"Hard to tell from here," Betsy said. "Why didn't you go talk to her? Seems stupid to come all this way and do nothing."

"I called her."

"Yeah, and look where that got ya." She snorted as she plucked a twig from my hair. "Want me to do it?"

"No!" Spoke too soon: Betsy's evil self had returned.

"Oooh, but now I really think I should," Betsy said.

"Betsy, please!"

But it was too late, Betsy was skipping merrily toward my mom. She looked back at me and smiled.

I dove behind the tree and watched. Yes, I know I could've just run up there with Betsy, but I didn't. It was pathetic. Anyway, they were too far away for me to hear what was going on, but I could see the Oscar-worthy performance Betsy was attempting to give. At least, I hoped Betsy was giving a performance; it would be much, much worse if she was telling my mom the truth.

Betsy was giving her a big, fake smile, of course, and her hands were whipping through the air like she was conducting a symphony. My mom's reaction was not so grand. She had one eyebrow raised—an expression that looked eerily familiar to me—and a scowl. She said a few words and waved her arm at Betsy, trying to get her to leave. Betsy persisted and gestured toward me! Mom held her hand above her eyes, trying to see me, but I couldn't tell if she succeeded. Betsy stepped toward Mom, who quickly stood up and said something that caused Betsy to cover her mouth in complete shock. Then Betsy slowly backed away from her.

I was on the verge of a heart attack by the time Betsy finally made it back to me.

"What happened?!" I blurted out as I pulled Betsy behind the tree. "Did she threaten you? Did you tell her I was here? Did you tell her I was here? Did she zap you or something? SPEAK!" My hands were shaking and I could feel my eyes bugging out of their sockets.

"Whoa, whoa, whoa!" Betsy put her hands up defensively. "Don't blow a fuse or, you know, blow us up!"

She had a good point. I didn't want my superpowers to go off again. I tried to take it down a notch.

"I can tell you this," Betsy said. "Your mom is not human."

"What?!" I grabbed her wrist.

With the most serious expression I had ever seen, Betsy said, "It's true. I'm sorry. Your mom can't be human. She wouldn't buy any Girl Scout cookies."

She snorted and whipped her arm away from me.

I knew if I said anything I would start to cry, so I didn't. Luckily, the bus arrived at that moment.

After one glance back at my mom—who was staring off into the distance—I got on board along with Betsy.

Betsy sat behind me and gave my seat a good kick. "Listen," she said, "I pretended to be selling cookies to try to get her name and address. She definitely is your mom."

I turned around and looked at her.

"Oh, geez. Don't frickin' cry about it." She sighed. "But she also doesn't have an address. She's 'just visiting.'"

"Just visiting?"

"Yeah, that's what she said before she went all screamy on me. That lady could really use a cookie." There was a long pause before Betsy added, "Actually, I think your mom and my mom would hit it off."

# CHAPTER FOURTEEN
## SPLITTING UP

I had timed my arrival back home like a professional school skipper. Not too shabby for my first time. Dad had already gone back to work after lunch, which was perfect because I desperately needed to lie down. Trying to find my mom had just made me feel worse and more confused. I'd found her, sure, but I couldn't work up the guts to talk to her. How could I ever expect to be anyone important if I couldn't even talk to my own mother? All these things, whether it was becoming an Est or fixing my powers, were just getting harder and less likely to happen. I hated feeling so helpless and small. There were so many things I wanted to be, but not a single one of them was the mess I saw in the mirror. Why couldn't I just be Artiest already? *Why*? At least then I would have one place where I actually belonged.

My head spun. I sat on the edge of my desk and waited for the dizziness to pass.

Einstein had wandered into the room and was making a bed out of this morning's towel and a sweatshirt. Happy as a clam, he picked up the towel in his mouth and rearranged it into a mangled, uncomfortable-looking pile and then plopped his fuzzy body down like he'd found the fluffiest cloud in the sky. I joined him, resting my cheek on the wood floor. The cool surface felt good. I was so tired.

Tired? Was I tired? A weird giggle popped out of my mouth. Did I just giggle? It sounded nothing like me. My stomach was really queasy. Was I going to throw up? I couldn't tell. Without warning, my arm swung out and smacked against the leg of my desk. Ow! Wait, did that hurt? Was I angry? My brain was in such a fog that I couldn't tell down from up. Maybe I just needed to close my eyes. Just for a second . . .

When I opened my eyes, the first thing I noticed was that I was back sitting on the edge of my desk. Hadn't I been on the floor with Einstein? Maybe I had just imagined that. My head was now cool to the touch, but my face was wet, like I'd been crying.

I went to look in the mirror. Other than the tear-streaked face, I looked normal. No stupidpowers poking out. Something felt off, though. *Really* off. I had this urge to get my sketchbook, but I wasn't sure why. I didn't have anything in particular that I wanted to draw. I reached into my backpack, and that's when I saw what was wrong. My hand, my arm—I looked back into the mirror to see my side view.

I was thin! Not like supermodel thin, but flat, like a cartoon character that had been smooshed by a steam-roller. Suddenly, my hands twitched and I couldn't control them. Without any sort of rational thought, I sat down and my hand started sketching. It was like my hand had a mind of its own! With lightning speed, it drew Keesha and me. Or, at least, it kinda looked like me—but much sportier. Keesha and the sportier me were running in the gym and looked like best friends.

My other hand whipped the page over and started on a clean sheet of paper. Again, I was drawing me, but this time with Hun Su in the school bathroom, and I was a beautiful, air-brushed version of myself with pouty lips and long lashes. We were trying on makeup together.

*Again*, my hand flipped to a new page and started to draw. The sketch looked like one of the science labs at school. A smarter, glasses-wearing version of me was at the board writing calculations while Kate looked on, completely astounded. As I imagined her congratulating me on my brilliance, my hand drifted to the side of the paper to add something to the scene. It was Charlie, peeking into the classroom.

"*Oh-oh-ah-ah!*" sounded out in the room, startling me. It was the monkey ringtone that signaled Charlie was calling. My hands still wouldn't obey me, but I managed to hit the Accept button with my toe, then mashed at the screen with it until I hit the Speaker button.

"H-how are you doing that?" he replied. He sounded totally freaked out.

"Waddya mean?"

"I am looking at you right now and you aren't talking on the phone!" He sounded like he was yelling through gritted teeth.

I whipped my head around and scanned the windows. Where was he? "I'm on speaker, dude. Chill out!"

"Why are you at school?" he continued. "And why are you wearing glasses?"

My hands, unbidden, sketched in a cell phone into Charlie's hands, and added gritted teeth to his mouth.

Suddenly it all made sense. Wonderful, awful, horrible, brilliant, awful (did I already say that?), awful sense. The reason I was deflated, the reason I was sketching all these scenes—I had split into three more people. These scenes weren't imaginary—they were actually happening! Three more very real, living versions of myself: a sportier Veronica, a more popular Veronica, and a smarter Veronica. And the real me was what was left behind—a paper-thin version of myself.

The most epic stupidpower of stupidpowers.

I must've still had some kind of bond with those versions of me that made me sketch out what was actually happening to them at the same time as I sketched it. Because I still seemed to know what the other Veronicas were doing. Well, sort of, anyway.

Whoa.

"Veri?" Charlie said. I had been quiet too long.

My hand was gearing up for another sketch. With a

fresh page and frantic pencil, I went for it. This was something big. I could feel it.

"It—that's not me, Charlie. I'm at home. Stupid-powers!"

"What?" Charlie asked.

I tried to drag the phone closer, but all I managed to do was accidentally hit the End Call button with my foot.

My hand drew again, this time creating a Cool Veronica who was at the park with Blake. Cool Veronica smiled all kinds of casual. She was so cool. Right now, some piece of me was really hanging out with Blake and not being a big dork.

Back in my actual house, I felt woozy. My guess was that there wasn't much left of me to create these manifestations. A look at my hand proved me right; I was now so paper thin that it was almost transparent.

My vision was blurry and my head felt heavy.

Next thing I knew, Charlie was shaking me. "Veri!"

I must have fainted. I sat up and Charlie grabbed the still-open sketchbook from the desk and slammed it shut. Instantly, I felt better.

"What? What? What?" I heard myself say as I tried to pull my focus back to reality.

Charlie poked at my arm. "You're getting back to normal from . . . whatever you were before."

I could use my limbs again. I turned to the mirror. My profile confirmed it. I was reinflating.

I quickly explained what had happened—somehow with only minor interruptions from Charlie. I think he was too shocked to say more.

He flipped through my sketchbook. "So there were drawings of alternate Veronicas in here? Like the one I saw?"

"Yeah, that really happened."

"There isn't anything like that in here now." Charlie held up the book. All my alternate-self sketches were gone; they must have disappeared when he slammed the sketchbook shut. I hoped that meant all my other selves had disappeared as well.

"Maybe that smart one stuck around, and she can take your finals for you," he joked.

"Charlie, that's a brilliant idea."

Charlie stared at me like I was crazy.

But I kept going. "I could be anything I wanted, Charlie. Heck, all I have to do—"

"Is let your alternate selves live your life for you while you hide in here and flatten down to nothing?"

"Yes!" It was so simple.

"You've lost it, girlie. If you're being serious, then it's time to get some professional help."

"Oh, Charlie, you're blowing this way out of proportion."

"Me? *I'm* blowing things out of proportion? You're okay with having actual split personalities, and *I'm* the one with the problem?"

"Hey, that's not fair. I didn't ask for this to happen to me. Besides, what do you know about problems?" I tried to control my anger as my voice went up a few octaves.

"Problems aren't the SFC or Blakey-freaking-wakey!" he shouted. "Do you even remember what these other Veronicas were doing? What good is living a life that you can't remember? You are being so stupid that you're not even living your own life, Veri!"

Stupid? That was it. I shouted right back at him. "I know you don't care that you're an outcast, but I do! I can't help it if you don't care that no one likes you or that you don't belong anywhere!"

For a brief, awful moment I regretted what I'd just said.

"You're right," he said. "I don't care that I'm not an Est, because you know what? Those people are idiots. Mindless little robot people."

I bit my tongue. There were lots of things I wanted to say back, but I didn't want any more stupidpowers today. It had gotten a lot easier just to suppress my emotions instead of feeling them. Suppress for success!

"That's what you really want, then?" Charlie said. "To be someone who would never be friends with a guy like me?"

"How can you say that?"

"It's true!"

"Then leave," I said.

"My pleasure!"

I couldn't see how upset he was, but I could hear it as he stomped toward the door. And I heard him pause right before opening it. "You know, I don't know what makes me feel dumber: the fact that I never noticed how shallow you are or the fact that all this time I thought we were best friends." He paused, then said, "Since we were little kids I've only needed one person to like me."

He left without a look back.

# CHAPTER FIFTEEN
## MAKE UP OR BREAK UP

The dance was less than a week away, and boy, was there a lot of work to do. And I mean *a lot*. I was back to being normal sized and hadn't seen (or drawn) any of my Alties— my new term for my alternate selves—so they must have all disappeared. It was a relief, but also scary. All my Alties had made great impressions on the other Ests, not to mention Blake. Impressions that I now had to keep up.

Even though it was Sunday, I was headed out to plan the layout of the decorations when Hun Su texted me to come over to her place. Decorations could wait.

Hun Su greeted me at the door of her house, which was just as adorable as she was; a pale-blue cottage that even had a white picket fence. She was makeup-free but still looked beautiful and poreless.

"You can do my makeup today, right?" she asked hopefully as she led me to her room.

My Pretty Altie was a makeup expert, I remembered. Regular Veronica, definitely not.

Then she noticed I didn't look nearly as good today.

"You seem . . . really tired." she said. "Didn't you have time for makeup today? It's Sunday."

"I—uh, I'm really busy getting the dance stuff ready," I explained.

"I totally understand. But could you just do my face really quickly? Please? We're going to audition the final bands for the dance today and I want to look hot."

"I don't know . . ."

"Pretty please, Veronica? I'll love you forever!" She giggled.

What I should have done is made a better excuse, put my foot down, or even faked a sudden and severe illness, but instead I decided to try. I had watched tons of tutorials online. It looked *so* easy!

Hun Su had all her makeup organized in a panda-shaped box (cute, right?) and had set a chair in front of her full-length

mirror as our salon. A swipe of concealer, a dash of lip-
stick, and some eye shadow. I could handle those . . . kinda.
Then there's the eyeliner aspect of the whole beauty world.
Or, as I like to call it, the Eye Gouger.

"Let's get to it!" I said, with forced enthusiasm.

The foundation went on smearier than I thought it
would—or could. I wasn't allowed to use foundation yet,
so my skills were more like spills. Just getting an even layer
on her face used a lot of makeup. It looked pretty thick, so
I decided to add extra blush to give her face more dimen-
sion. Contouring, I think it's called. Eyeshadow: aces. Now
eyeliner. I was super cautious when I started tracing around
her eye. Maybe too cautious. When I stepped back to see
how the right eye had gone, it was painfully obvious that I
was afraid of poking her in the eye—the liner was really
far away from the target. Like I had just drawn a circle
around it.

"How's it looking? Cute?" She was bubbling over with
anticipation. She tried to sneak a peek in the mirror, but I
blocked her view.

"Uh, yeah! Cutest thing evahhh," I lied. "*Ummm*," I
thought as I spoke, "what do you think about a smoky eye?
It would be really grown-up!"

"Yes!" Hun Su squealed. She was getting giddy.

A smoky eye! I could just fill in the space between the liner and her lashes.

"Oh, Veronica! You should *totally* do our makeup for the dance!"

*Oh boy.* "Um, yeah . . . maybe," I mumbled as I worked.

"Are you bringing that Russian kid from school?"

Russian kid? "Oh! You mean Charlie. He's British. Not Russian. Well, actually, he's not even British."

"He's cute . . . in an interesting way." She opened her eyes wide for me to put mascara on her. "But it might be time for an upgrade! At least it's a group date, so you won't be stuck alone with him all night."

What was she talking about? A group date? With Blake?

Hun Su's phone buzzed. "It's Jenny. Let's send her a selfie."

"Not yet, not yet," I begged. I still needed to fix this mess.

"Ooh, drama!" She winked at me. "I'll just text her back and let her know we are busy getting pretty."

Her phone buzzed again almost immediately.

"What did Jenny say?" I was hopeful she was warming up to yours truly.

"Nothing." Hun Su grinned, but she didn't look that happy.

Her phone buzzed a few more times, causing Hun Su to sigh deeply before she set it facedown on the floor.

"Let me see," she playfully demanded as she grabbed my arm.

I stepped back to look at the finished product. *Gulp.*

Hun Su stared into the mirror. "I, uh . . ."

Again, she put on a fake smile and picked her phone back up. This time her feigned happiness was much more muted. She was trying to be polite.

"Thanks, Veronica," she nodded as she unceremoniously started herding me toward the door. Were there tears in her eyes? The makeup wasn't *that* bad! Okay, maybe it was.

On the way to the front door, Hun Su was texting wildly.

"Everything okay? Are you happy with the makeup?" I heard myself ask even though I knew the answer.

"Um, yeah," Hun Su said.

I tried to lighten things up. "Talking to Jenny? Anything going on? Did she buy another gold-plated phone case or something?"

"It's nothing," she said as she replied to another text. "Just a boy. Just a cute boy. You wouldn't understand."

"Text me?" I asked as I stepped out the door.

"See you later." Hun Su waved me off as she closed the door.

After that disaster, I decided to get to school to work on the decorations. I was much better with a paint brush than a blush brush.

On the way, I spotted Keesha putting on her shoes next to the track field. I hadn't really talked to her since she'd been kicked out of the SFC. (I wasn't counting whatever conversation she'd had with my sportstastic Altie.)

"Hey, you!" She beamed at me as she tightened up her sneakers.

"Hey!" I sat down next to her on the grass.

"No sitting, Speed Racer. Let's talk 'n' run!" She hopped up, clearly expecting me to follow her.

Halfway around the track, I was just about dead.

"Geez, what were you up to last night?" she joked over her shoulder.

"I think it's these shoes. And wearing regular clothes," I panted. "I'm not as aerodynamic! Also, I wanted to say I'm sorry you're not in the SFC anymore."

"Oh no! That's all over," she said with ease. "I'm back in now."

"Oh. That's cool." I huffed and puffed.

She ran backward so she could face me. "I heard you've joined us."

I managed an "Uh-huh."

"A word of caution," she offered. "Jenny doesn't like being second place. She didn't like it when Betsy was getting all those art awards, she didn't like that I was dating a high schooler, and I'm sure she's definitely jealous over how much everyone's starting to like you."

"What does that matter? She's still Richest."

"Believe me, it matters to her. She invited me back an hour after Mark dumped me." Keesha turned around and zoomed away. "She'll never want to share the spotlight!"

I was left in the dust.

# CHAPTER SIXTEEN
## BEAUTY SLEEP

By the end of school on Monday I was feeling really lonely. Charlie hadn't responded to my bajillion messages—even after I told him it was majorly important I hear from him. And, honestly, I had noticed the Ests were often too busy to talk, or they simply "didn't see me" when I was walking down the hall. Keesha might have been right—jealous Jenny was trying to keep me down.

I had stayed up late the night before to get as much prep work done for the dance as I could, but I had become preoccupied by something else super important. Okay, actually, I got fixated on whether I should text Blake to clarify what Hun Su had said about a group date to the dance. I wrote and erased texts for most of the night. I finally achieved this exchange:

**Me:** Hey, Veronica here! Things r getting pretty crazy, so I wanted to check in about the dance. So we're all going together, I guess? Need a ticket? ☺

[An hour later]

**Blake:** It's cool.
**Me:** Sounds great! Ride?
**Blake:** Yup. 7.

And that was it. At least I got a small bit of info from him?

When school was over for the day, I was exhausted. There was so much to be done, though, I had to push through and work on the decorations before I could sleep. I gave the janitor my student ID (complete with horrible photo) and the note from Mrs. Krenshaw that allowed me to be in the school after hours. The dude took his duties seriously. He stared at my ID, then at me, then back at my ID, shining his flashlight in my eyes repeatedly. Did I really look like trouble? I was a half-awake girl wearing a panda sweatshirt. After a series of questions that would put the TSA to shame, the janitor escorted me to the gym. The entire way. Because I might, you know, decide to do some after-hours algebra or something.

The gym was dark and strange at night. I flipped on the light switch, which made a heavy industrial *click*, much louder than the light switches at home. The large overhead lights flashed on with a buzzing sound I had never noticed before.

"Hello?" I said just to make sure I was alone.

Nothing.

I opened the supply closet, which Charlie had helped me fill with my supplies before he decided he hated me forever. It was packed with what an uninformed stranger might think were the remnants of a Halloween party at a dude ranch.

I dragged all that crap out of the closet and got to work on the main banner. It was a rather mammoth undertaking. Rolled into all the other things I had agreed to do, I had said yes to a banner that read HAY IS FOR HORSES & BLOOD IS FOR VAMPIRES!

It was one of what I had started to see were *many* poor

decisions. For one thing, the banner would need to be about the length of a whole gym wall!

Just outlining the letters took a few hours and really hurt my knees. I chugged down yet another soda and tried to pump myself up: "Come on, Veronica! This is going to be amazing! You and Blake are going to dance under this banner!" It worked, at least for a bit, and using the wrestling mats to kneel on was a pure-genius move, if I do say so myself. But about halfway through the coloring phase, I began to really struggle. And by "really struggle" I mean I fell asleep, face-planting right into some wet paint.

So tired. So very tired . . .

When I woke up, the morning light was hitting me directly in the face. Schnitzel! I bet Dad was freaking out. It was Tuesday morning and I had been at school all night. My phone was dead. I'd have to get my charger from my locker. And I had slept through valuable decoration-making time.

After wiping my drool off the wrestling mat, I made my way to my locker. No one was at school yet, but they soon would be, and I needed to make myself look like I hadn't slept here. I yawned. *Oooof!* And I needed to find some mints. ASAP!

Once my phone had a little juice, I saw an onslaught of messages from Dad. I sent him a text telling him I was sorry and explaining that I had fallen asleep in school. His response: *Don't get another detention.* Man, he was still really mad at me.

By the time everyone was at school, I felt like I had done a decent job of disguising my day-old ick. I covered up my top with my trusty old hoodie and still had a knit hat from winter jammed under my overdue library books. I would be hot, considering it was about seventy degrees outside, but at least no one would see my greasy hair.

The rest of the day was a lot busier than I imagined. My frazzled brain couldn't take much more. I was so happy when the bell rang, even though it meant I had to run immediately to the bloodsucking horses and switch my booty into hyperdrive. Getting all the decorations done by the next night was going to be nearly impossible, but I knew I could do it. I *had* to do it. There really wasn't much of an option at this point; if I didn't get it done, it would be an instant sentence to life in captivity, or, at least, high school at the loser table. Blake told me I was cool. Nothing, let me repeat, *nothing* was going to mess that up.

Waiting for me in the gym was Jenny and the rest of the SFC. I was really happy to see them (and hoped they had come to help) until I saw Jenny's expression.

"What's your deal, Veronica?" Jenny screeched.

"What's up, guys?" I smiled at them weakly. "I know I'm a little behind, but it's cool! Don't worry, the gym will blow your minds when I'm done."

"And you think you deserve to be one of us?" Jenny hissed. "You'd better pray for a miracle in the next twenty-four hours, Veronica."

Jenny stomped out of the gym, leaving scuffmarks and a very upset me in her wake. The others followed. Kate gave me an apologetic glance before she left and Keesha whispered, "I told you she couldn't handle it."

*Twenty-four hours.* Hearing it laid out like that, I realized how much I had left to do.

I was in full panic mode now. Who could I call to help? No one. I mean, really—no one. No one was speaking to me. Not Charlie, not my dad, certainly not the SFC. I couldn't ask Blake to help. How pathetic would that look? Besides, I wanted him to be wowed by all the work I had done, too. At school I was pretty much only friends with Charlie. I really didn't know anyone else. Except . . .

"See how I made the feng shui work here?" Ted mused as he helped me hang the banner during lunch. He was more than happy to help, telling me it was like "dollars in the karma bank." I worried getting Ted past the janitor would be hard, but it turns out the janitor filled up a "Pretzelentologist Frequent-Biter Card" every single week over at the pretzel stand. (For the record, that means ten pretzels a week.)

Ted had saved my butt by bringing leftover and frozen pretzels to help me fill the gaps in my food plan. I had baked and chopped vegetables and smooshed guacamole for most of the night, but the pretzels would ensure no one would have to dance hungry.

"Man, I have some great memories of this place," he said.

"I went to school with your dad," he said as I climbed down the ladder.

"High school, too." He paused to think. "He had some serious qi problems."

He must have seen the look on my face.

"Qi. It's like your life energy," he explained.

I couldn't help but laugh. "Yeah, my dad can be a little intense."

"That is also true," Ted agreed as he got ready to leave.

I had another question. "So, did you ever meet my mom?"

Ted nodded. "Sure did. We were lab partners senior year."

"Strange question: Do you think she was dangerous? My dad said she was."

"Nah." Ted scratched his head, mussing up his shaggy hair even more than usual. "Some people, though, have a hard time with 'weird.' Change freaks them out."

Dad did have a hard time when things didn't go according to plan. "But that doesn't mean weird is bad or dangerous."

"Of course not," he agreed. "Weird is wonderful. It makes the world go round."

It might have been a sign of my impending nervous breakdown, but that sounded comforting. Maybe Dad had just decided weird was bad. It didn't mean Mom was actually dangerous. It didn't mean I was dangerous. There was hope.

And this dance! It was really starting to shape up and look like "Equestrian Gothic." For real. I had taken a few artistic liberties that I was pretty darn proud of. The mash-up of horses and vampires came together in a Victorian theme with some Dracula-esque touches. Horses with red eyes pulled carriages. I'd spray painted bales of hay black and set up serving bowls of chips and pretzels in upside-down top hats.

A giddy rush swept through me, and my powers created a small fireworks show over my head. Luckily, Ted was too busy to notice, and I was able to make them quickly disappear.

"Thanks for the help, Ted!" I went to high-five him, but instead he offered his usual little bow. I course-corrected and pretended to adjust the collar of my shirt before quickly bowing back.

"Namaste, little bird. Looks like you have elsewhere to fly." He pointed toward the back wall. Betsy was helping tear down the art show. I had been so busy I had totally forgotten the art contest winners had been announced. I could see a blue ribbon hanging from each of Betsy's entries—first place in both categories. Ms. Brannon loved realism, for sure. Betsy caught my eye and smirked while patting her pocket with the memory card in it—clearly to remind me she still had photos of me mid-stupidpower. Great. That was another thing to worry about tonight. *Bleh*.

I watched Ted shuffle out the gym door, and then I took a moment to appreciate how freaking cool the gym looked.

The whole theme was very mysterious, which I thought would play well. Still, I was a little nervous through the rest of the school day, right up until the big truck of flowers arrived a few hours later. The delivery people loved my decorations. They called them *unique* and *creative*. The lady even said that she wished her school dances had been this cool.

My pride instantly took a blow when Jenny and Keesha decided to pop their heads in and see how things were going. Jenny didn't look nearly as impressed as I hoped she would.

"It's all right, I guess," she said.

"Are you kidding? It's amazing!" Keesha said. Jenny gave her a death glare.

"I worked really hard on it, so I hope you like it." I genuinely meant that.

"Well, it has my name on it, so I better like it," Jenny sneered.

"Excuse me?" On the other side of the gym I saw Betsy perk up. I'm sure she was loving this.

"I am the leader of the Ests, Veronica. I make or break the SFC and that includes you." Jenny strutted out of the gym. Keesha rolled her eyes and followed her.

I looked back at Betsy, but she'd bolted. I noticed there was still one piece of paper hanging on the wall where the art show had been. Walking over, I saw that the paper had been folded in half and pinned up with a tack. "Freak" was scrawled across it. *Hmmm.* Give ya one guess who left that.

I pried the tack out and as the paper unfolded, a camera's memory card fell to the ground. The piece of paper was a sketch Betsy had done of green-with-envy Veronica. Over the top Betsy had scrawled, "The only people I hate more than you are the Ests."

Considering our past, this felt like a love note. She'd

given me all the stupidpower pictures. All her evidence to turn me into a social outcast. I took the memory card and put it in my locker. I wouldn't dare take it home and have Dad find it. I needed to figure out how to dispose of it properly, and permanently.

For now, I was finally done with dance prep, and with two hours to spare. Yikes! I needed to rush home and get ready. At least the chaperones were in charge of getting the food out before the dance, giving me (and my hair) a few extra minutes to primp.

Despite the rush, the sight of my fancy dress made me smile. Sure, it was from Cashman's Outlet, not Chateau Chez. But I thought it was the most beautiful dress I had ever seen. It was navy with sequins and a black tulle over-lay. Like a sky full of stars.

Dolled up, I went downstairs. Even if dad was still cranky with me, I knew he needed to see this dress.

"Ta-da!" I cheered and did a little twirl as I went into the living room. (I only tripped a little.)

"*Yeowza!* That is a fancy potato sack," he said.

"Thank you, thank you." I bowed as if I had just won an Oscar; gracious, and yet completely full of myself.

"That's why it really sucks to have to tell you that you need to stay home," he said.

I laughed at his funny, funny, ridiculous joke.

"I'm serious, Veri. I'm sorry, but I'm serious."

"What did I do? I mean, recently?"

"Nothing," he said sadly.

"Then why?"

"Listen, I heard your mom came to the club yesterday when I wasn't there. I think she's gonna try to get you. You need to stay here with me where you'll be safe." He put his hands on my shoulders.

"Safe? Dad, she's not dangerous." My voice shook. I wondered if I should tell him that I went to see her, but decided I shouldn't because: "If you think she's dangerous, then I'd hate to see what you thought of me if—"

*HONK-HONK!*

"My ride is here. I'm going." I tried to turn away, but his grip on my shoulders stopped me.

"No, Veronica!" he commanded.

"This isn't fair!" I yelled up to his face. I could feel my own anger growing like a fire inside me.

*"Oww!"* Dad threw his hands off my shoulders and looked at them.

I knew what had happened: my anger had activated my powers. And, as usual when I'm angry, fiery heat had come. My skin had become so hot, it burned my dad's hand.

"Veri?"

I was already out the door.

# CHAPTER SEVENTEEN
## MYSTERY DATE

"Hi, guys!" I said as cheerfully as possible as I squeezed into the backseat of the minivan next to Blake.

Kate's oldest brother, Jim, was driving his sister, me, Blake, and Keesha to the dance.

"Hey, Veronica!" Kate said. "That dress is amazing!"

"Oh, thanks!" I said.

"Totally sweet," Blake confirmed.

I was determined to enjoy the night. Sure, Jenny wasn't happy with me, but I had to hope she'd chill out once she had some fun at the dance. I didn't want to step on anyone's toes, but I *did* want to get my Est title. Come on, I'd literally torn myself apart dealing with my superpowers and working my butt off to get to this moment. Tonight was my night, and no one was going to take it from me.

FYI, I wasn't at all worried about Mom showing up for multiple reasons:

1. How would she recognize me? It had been twelve years.
2. If Dad's big fear was her "dangerous" powers, I already knew more about them than he did.
3. I knew what she looked like, thanks to my bus trip to Westchester, so I'd see her coming.

Jim pulled up to school and let us out at the curb. I rifled around in my pockets to find my ticket as we walked up the stairs.

"That dress has pockets?" Blake asked.

"Yes! Deciding factor," I admitted. "I can't do purses, I forget them everywhere."

He smiled. "There she is." He was looking at Hun Su, who was giddily waving at him. (Her makeup was flawless, btw.)

"See ya later?" Blake punched me lightly in the shoulder, like I was one of his dude buddies. Then he rushed up the stairs two at a time and straight to Hun Su. They hugged, and she held onto his arm as they went inside.

What just happened? I stopped on the stairs. Kate patted me on the back as she and Keesha followed them in.

I felt a light mist on my face. *Not now, stupidpowers. Please, not now.* A slight fog had formed over my head, threatening rain. Quickly, I waved my hand through it, breaking it up. My heart felt so fragile and sore. *Veronica McGowan, you're not cool.*

Sadness was starting to engulf me. I needed to talk myself out of it before my powers went haywire.

It was time for a pep talk of epic proportions.

*This is just a little setback. Don't worry about it. Remember when Blake wasn't part of the equation? When getting Artiest was everything you wanted? You can still do that. You can still get that Est! You did the best job ever on decorations! Own it!*

My fragile feeling didn't go away completely, but the chances of rain went down to normal. I had this under control.

Until I noticed some familiar red hair sitting on the top step, waiting for me.

"Veronica?" my mom asked, cocking her head to one side and squinting.

"That's me," I answered, but I didn't move any closer to her.

Just like before, seeing Mom didn't feel good. Something was missing. I should have felt an instant bond, especially since we shared the same affliction, but instead I wanted to run in the opposite direction. Or maybe it was just Dad's voice echoing through my head, telling me not to trust her. My stomach started to hurt. It felt like something was moving around in there. I put my hand on my belly. Sure enough, my stomach was literally tying in knots! I cringed and tried my best to ignore it. I'd been packing the emotions in so tightly it was starting to feel like I might burst.

"How do you know what I look like?" I asked.

"You know who I am?" She was surprised.

I nodded.

"Well, I saw you on TV," she answered. "The fire at school."

*How many times did they replay that news report?*

She offered me her hand. It was small and looked harmless enough, but I stepped away from her and she dropped it. Why didn't this feel okay?

"You sent me that article, didn't you?" I asked. "You wanted me to know about the superpowers."

"Yes. It was time you knew the truth. Setting fire to your school was proof." She reached out again. "Come with me."

I had so many questions. Questions that needed answering before we went any farther. I was so mad at Dad, but darned if he hadn't made me a naturally suspicious person—and for once it seemed appropriate. "Where have you been? Did someone cure you?" I asked quietly.

"Cure me?" She sounded confused. "You're the one who needs to be cured. I don't care what your father says." She latched onto my wrist.

"What?"

"Your dad is a menace, Veronica. He's unfit to be a parent!"

I went to pull my hand away, but she was holding my wrist as tightly as she could.

"Let me go!" I yelled. "My dad may work two jobs and smoke cigars and make everyone afraid of him, but"—this is where I realized I wasn't making the point I needed to—"who are you to say anything about him?! You've been gone my whole life and now you show up? Because we are both freaks?" I could feel my stupidpowers firing up.

"Ow!" Mom whipped her hand away and blew on it. I looked at my wrist; it was glowing like red-hot metal.

I needed to get away from my mom before this got any worse.

"Hey!" Ms. Watson shouted, hurrying toward us from inside the dance. She must have seen what looked like an attempted abduction. (And it sort of was exactly that.)

A giant scowl took over Ms. Watson's face when she spotted Mom. "You!"

"Agent Hendriks?" My mom looked just as disgusted.

"Agent Hendriks?" I echoed.

Ms. Watson/Agent Hendriks ushered us both behind a pine tree at the bottom of the stairs.

"This woman made our lives a living hell after the first storm, Veronica," Mom said. "Told everyone she could that we were a family of weirdos. All for her career."

"You're a government agent?" I stared at my guidance counselor in shock.

"I was a pretty high-ranking one," she said, "until your father started filing complaints against me. Then I became one of the most laughed-at agents in the bureau. A conspiracy nut."

"So you came back to prove you were right?" I side-stepped my mom. "You knew I had superpowers all along?"

"Yes," Ms. Watson said. "Another McGowan in the middle of suspicious activity certainly caught my eye."

"What now?" I asked. "You're going to turn me in? Save your reputation?"

"Well, I just got fired, so now I'm a full-time guidance counselor and nothing else," Ms. Watson said.

"Being an agent was your other job?" I asked.

Mom stepped up. "Not to worry, *former* Agent Hendriks. I'm going to turn Veronica in."

"What?" I shouted, backing away.

"You're going to get help, Veronica," Mom said.

"Help?" I asked. "What does that mean?"

Ms. Watson answered, " 'Help' is an interesting way of putting it. From what I know, you'd go to a place where they wouldn't help you—but you'd help them. You have a lot of power, Veronica. Power certain people want to tap into."

This was bad. This was really, really bad.

I looked at Mom. "What? You'd let people experiment on me?"

"It's all for the greater good," Mom said.

"No. You're supposed to protect me!" I tried to run away, but Ms. Watson blocked my path.

"Watch out, she's hot to the touch," Mom warned Ms. Watson, waving her burned hand.

Now both my arms were heating up, right out here in front of everyone. I was grasping at straws, looking for a hero. "Ms. Watson, or whatever your name is, you have to help me," I pleaded.

My mom smirked.

"There comes a time," Ms. Watson said, "when we have to be brave. No matter what will come of it."

"But . . . you're my guidance counselor!"

Ms. Watson stepped between Mom and me. She took a moment to really think while she looked back and forth between us. I was sure doom was near.

"You're right," Ms. Watson said. "I *am* your guidance counselor now, and it's my job to help you."

*Did I just hear her right?*

"Veronica, go inside while I deal with your mother."

*Holy baloney, I did!* The look on my mom's face was priceless. At least for a second, before thoughts started rushing back into my brain. This lady was my mom. My *mom.* The person I'd been pining for all these years. And she was nothing like I thought she'd be. I wanted to say something else. Something mean, but nothing came to mind.

"Go!" Ms. Watson swatted at me.

I ran. Looking over my shoulder, I saw Ms. Watson try to look nonchalant as she ushered Mom into a car.

Once I was in the school, my first inclination was to call Charlie.

*"This is Charles Weathers, Esquire. I accept small bills, money orders, and voice mails."* BEEP!

"Charlie, it's, uh, me. Something really weird just happened and . . . I don't know. I need to talk to someone, and you were the first person I thought of who would, you know, listen. Um, my mom was here and Ms. Watson is totally a government agent. Soooo, yeah. Call me. Please."

I hung up and took a few breaths. My arms had cooled down. I had to get myself together before I went into that gym. If I tried my best to be positive, there really wasn't anything worse that could happen tonight, right? Having your crappy mom decide to send you in for vivisection pretty much tops the crappy list. Add to it that your crush is crushing on someone else, and your dad and your best friend hate your guts. So, things couldn't get worse. The rest of the night could still be magical.

I found the Ests and Blake behind the band's stage, waiting to make their grand entrance and, I dunno, maybe give a speech or something.

To be fair, Blake and Hun Su looked cute together. *I should tell them that*, I thought. I smiled, but they were all giving me funny looks. Kate had covered her mouth with her hands while Keesha comforted her.

Titan, looking worried, approached me. "You should really see a doctor, Veronica."

Before I could ask him what he meant, Jenny linked arms with me and whispered, "I admit, I was kinda worried you'd be hard to take down, since everyone seems to really like you, but it turns out you are lot weirder than I could ever have hoped for."

With that she opened my hand and dropped my locker's padlock in my palm. It had been cut open!

"Your public awaits," she snickered before she shoved me through the curtain and onto the stage.

The Goth band stopped playing and someone swung a spotlight on me, causing everyone to turn and look. Some were wide-eyed. Some laughed; some looked downright terrified. What was happening? My eyes adjusted to the lights and I looked behind me. I gasped. Suddenly I couldn't breathe. The projector wasn't rotating through photos of Victorian England like it was supposed to; it was rotating through photos of me with all my stupidpowers! There I was: green with envy, on the porch with a rain cloud over my head, being thrown backward by an invisible punch, and others, each more embarrassing than the last.

The Ests had gone into my locker and found the memory card with all of Betsy's photos. Photos of me. Photos of my powers.

Then the chanting started:

*"Weirdest! Weirdest! Weirdest!"*

I wanted to run off the stage, but I couldn't. It was like my legs were stuck to the floorboards. I had no choice but to take the abuse because, well, I believed it. I was Weirdest. Every single dream I'd ever had was shattered. Every single person I wanted to be, all my new friends thought I was a freak. What's worse is that they were right.

Seeing all the pictures sealed the deal.

Nothing could change it now.

It was time to let it all out.

# CHAPTER EIGHTEEN
## IT'S MY PARTY AND I'LL DESTROY IT IF I WANT TO

All the emotions I had been keeping in? They were about to burst. There were so many, I couldn't settle on one. The changes from anger to sadness to relief were happening so quickly that the room began to spin. I closed my eyes, feeling my stupidpowers rise up, each fighting the other to be dominant. I didn't have any strength or will left in me to fight them. I was a lost cause and I knew it.

I felt a whoosh of wind and opened my eyes. My powers had manifested in a swirling, colorful tornado that seemed to contain all my feelings. There was fire, thunder, lightning, and rain all mixed together. The tornado whipped through the room, destroying everything in its path. Guacamole splattered against the wall; the decorations I had worked so hard on were catching on fire and flipping violently through the air. Tables and chairs flipped over and everyone ran for cover.

Blake and Hun Su made it all the way to the door. I couldn't believe that just minutes ago I thought they looked cute together. They weren't my friends. They probably knew this was happening and did nothing. At the very least, they didn't try to help me.

Something that I can only call laser beams shot out of my eyes, sealing the gym door shut. Blake and Hun Su shook uselessly at the handles.

"Veronica! Stop it!" Jenny screeched from behind a toppled cardboard horse.

"You stop it!" I stomped up to her and used my now-flaming hand to turn the horse into ash. Jenny screamed. "You think you're better than everyone else!" I yelled at her. "You aren't! You're worse!"

I took another step toward Jenny, who was now crab walking away from me. "I can't believe I ever wanted to be like you," I shouted. "Like any of you!" I gestured to the other Ests. I didn't know what I was going to do next; I had never felt such an excruciating wave of feelings. It was

like I didn't control my body anymore. My emotions did. And I could see the fear in Jenny's eyes.

Even worse, I liked it.

"Yo, Veri!"

Snapped out of my ragey trance, I turned to see my dad, braving the Veronica-made storm. Suddenly things felt more real, saner. For some reason, this was the first thing that popped out of my mouth: "Dad? Mom was here! She wanted to take me away!"

"I know!" He jumped up onstage and grabbed my shoulder.

"I hate her! I hate her so much!" I screamed. I couldn't help it. "She did this to me! Then she left us!"

The tornado intensified. The other kids were grabbing onto anything that was bolted down so they wouldn't be swept away. Rain poured, pulling down what was left of the crepe paper. A gigantic bolt of lightning flashed, destroying the chandeliers.

"She's the reason I'm a freak!" I cried as the tornado ate up everything in sight.

"No, sweetie." My dad grabbed my other shoulder and pulled me around to face him. I'd never seen his face like this before. My dad actually looked . . . scared.

"It's not her. Whatever you are, I was, too."

His words whipped into the back of my brain. My brain wasn't processing the words, but my body knew. At the same time, a crackling noise shot through the gym and the scene froze. I mean, I *actually froze* everything in the room. The kids, the tornado, the horribly wonderful Goth band, all were completely silent. Everything was encased in a thick sheet of ice, except Dad and me.

"What?" I asked quietly.

"You had the powers when you were a baby, but they went away. Just like mine eventually did. Just like your grandma's did and Great-Grandma Beatrice's did. I saw the signs that yours were back, but I didn't want to believe it. I didn't want to think about the problems they could cause us."

"And Mom?"

"Your mom threatened to leave if we didn't hand you over to the government. I told her if she left she could never come back." Dad shook his hand like it had fallen asleep. A trail of blue lines on his fingers showed how my iciness had started to seep into him. He, too, was starting to freeze, but he didn't fully let go of me, despite the fact that he was about to become a real-life Frosty the Snowman.

"And you never told me?" I asked. My voice was getting stronger and fiercer as the cold inched its way up his arm.

"She got freaked out after that storm we caused when you were a baby. She wanted to turn us in. She wanted to separate us. I wouldn't let that happen." His voice cracked. "There was an ultimatum. I don't do ultimatums."

"You knew I was messed up!" I raged. "All these years! You *knew*! And you lied about Mom. You are the one who said we don't keep things from each other!"

His eyes were starting to glisten, but I knew it wasn't from having an icicle arm.

I was glad.

"I just wanted to keep you safe," he said.

"Safe?" In the midst of all this destruction, did he just say *safe*?

That's when something inside me broke. My fragile heart cracked and splintered, then fell to the bottom of the darkest pit in my soul. I had given up so much to become an Est. Charlie hated me, and my dad, whom I loved and trusted more than any person on earth, had kept this from me, had lied to me all these years. I was alone. And that's how it was going to be from here on out. I couldn't recover from this. No one would want to be my friend, not even me. I was insignificant, I was worthless, and I *was* Weirdest.

Or worse, I didn't even exist.

"Veronica," Dad whispered. I could tell he was trying to reach me, but it was too late. I was gone. I could feel it.

I exhaled as hard as I could, which released a huge shock wave through the gym. It broke up all the ice, which crackled and shattered as it fell off everything and everyone. The wave smashed into the walls with such force they fell down. Only the wall that attached the gym to the rest of the school was left standing. And me.

Reality check: I just wailed on everyone with my stupidpowers!

Was anyone hurt? I rushed over to Dad, who had been knocked off his feet, but he looked fine; then I jumped off the stage and began checking on everyone else. My shock wave had hit them, but it seemed like they were all okay. How was that even possible? Some were rubbing their eyes like they had just woken up.

Then I realized that for the first time in a long time, I felt . . . okay. All those pent-up emotions were gone, purged from the inside out. Everything was quite literally out in the open, and there was nothing I could do about it. I had to face my so-called superpowers. More than likely, I'd have to face them in a padded cell or with needles being constantly jabbed in me, but who cares? I'd lost everything, so what did I have to save? Maybe I was Weirdest, and maybe that was as good as it got.

I reached down to help Jenny, ready for her to threaten me with lawyers and exile to the front of the bus.

Instead she held out her arm and gladly accepted my hand as she stood. "Holy cow!" she exclaimed. "That was, like, bananas."

"Yeah, I'm sorry," I said. "Things got really out of control."

Titan sauntered over, rubbing his head, which had a pretty big scrape. "Isn't that the whole point of nature? It's never under control."

"Uh, Titan, I think we need to check you for head trauma," I said. Why was he talking about nature?

He gave me a puzzled look. "How do you know my name?"

Oh, crap. His brain must be mush! My powers turned his brain to MUSH.

"Here. Sit down," I said, turning a chair right side up. "I'll get my dad to check you out. He knows a thing or two about bodily harm."

I went back to the stage and found Dad sitting on the edge.

"Dad! I think Titan might have a concussion." I motioned for him to follow me. He didn't get up. Instead he just raised an eyebrow at me.

*"Dad?"* he asked. He took a good, long look at me before he shook his head violently, as if he was clearing out some cobwebs. "Yeah, Veronica. Veronica. I'm your dad."

We found Titan, who was now surrounded by the Ests.

"Oh, hey, Doctor McGowan," Titan said. "I'm fine. I think that maybe this girl got hit on the head." He pointed at me.

Me? This girl?

"I'm Veronica. Guys?" They all gave me blank expressions. "I go to school with you? I helped plan this dance?"

"Oh, yeah!" Derek smiled. "You're in fifth grade or something . . ."

"Hey, Rik, could you check me?" Blake asked. His perfect hair had been flattened and he was obviously shaken.

"Sure." Dad found nothing physically wrong with Blake, but I was less than impressed with their conversation.

"So, Rik, how's life?" Blake asked.

"Can't complain. Except for the part where you call me Rik."

"Right, right. Hey, Veronica! Long time no see." Blake looked back at my dad. "Middle school kids, am I right?"

He was in middle school last year, thank you very much. Besides, was he really trying to look cool to my dad? The layers were peeling back from Blake. Right now he just looked like a high school freshman with bad hair, desperate to seem cool. Yuck. I wasn't sure if it was good or bad that this was the least disturbing revelation of the day.

"Man, I wish I had some lip balm," Blake added.

I reached into my dress pocket and grabbed a tube.

"No way! Your dress has pockets?!" he asked.

"Yeah, still does."

Amid my confusion, Dad gently pulled me aside.

"Kiddo."

"Dad," I replied. I couldn't look him in the eye.

"I'm so, so sorry. I know it doesn't mean much right now, but I thought I was doing the right thing. It was stupid.

I'm on your case constantly about the truth and here I, the adult, screwed it all up."

"I'm sorry, too. Everyone hates me. I destroyed the stupid dance. I should have told you everything that was happening."

He nodded. "I think today we learned that everyone makes mistakes. Even adults."

"What's gonna happen to me now, Dad?" I forced myself to look up at him. "Bad things, right? I don't think I can change this—this thing about me."

"No. And I wouldn't want you to. And maybe one day you won't want to, either."

"Doubtful."

"Anyway, I think ya lucked out—it seems like your little wave of preteen self-loathing made them forget you." He gave me a sympathetic look. "But seriously, look at them. Maybe it's for the best."

Hun Su was dusting Blake off like a prized antique. (But they still looked cute together, especially now that I didn't like him so much.) Jenny and Derek were fixing Kate's hair, while Keesha stretched and ran in place. I looked at them—I really looked at *them*. Why had I only seen the things they had that I wanted? Every single one of them was ter-

rified of Jenny, who bossed them around constantly. I wish
her parents' fortune could buy her a surgery to take out her
bossy bone. I might not be Prettiest or Richest, but I'm
also not Meanest or Scardiest (let's pretend that's a word),
and that was something I could handle. Something I could
be proud of.

# CHAPTER NINETEEN
## ALL'S WELL THAT ENDS KINDA OKAY

Dad and I checked on everyone else. One by one, students and chaperones all confirmed they were okay—and they had never seen yours truly before. EVER. In fact, none of them remembered my powers, what had happened, or me. "Another freak storm" seemed to be the phrase of the day.

"So, why do you remember me?" I asked Dad. We could hear the sirens of police cars and fire engines making their way to the school.

"At first I had no clue who you were, but I came around. You are my daughter, ya know."

I hugged him, but my brief joy was snatched away

when I spotted a natural redhead motionless under a table. It was Charlie!

"No!" I ran to Charlie, and Dad easily lifted the table off of him. "Charlie!" I shouted in his face. "Charlie! Are you okay? What are you doing here?"

I was so relieved to see him. Then I realized the worst thing ever: Charlie wouldn't know who I was. His memory would be wiped clean of me, just like everyone else's.

"He is one tough little dude, isn't he?" Dad said as Charlie opened his eyes.

"Well, it keeps me original," he coughed out.

Sure, since he wouldn't know me, the bear hug I gave him might have seemed creepy, but I didn't care. He was okay. I didn't murder my best friend. Er, former best friend.

"I'm sorry. I'm so sorry," I said, letting go of him.

Charlie sat up and scratched his head. "It's okay. I got your message and decided not to hate you anymore." He straightened his dance bow tie. "Look at this mess, Veri!"

My eyes welled up. "You know who I am?"

"Yeah?" He lifted one eyebrow at me, then looked at my dad. "So, you know everything now?"

Dad nodded. "I think so. Turns out she got her powers from me. Surprise."

Charlie beamed. "That's the coolest thing ever! You guys need to fight crime or something. How cool is that?"

"You know who I am!" I couldn't get over it. I bounced up and down.

Charlie stared at me. "Wait. Do other people *not* know who you are?"

"Yeah, that's a side effect this time, I guess."

"Then everything is back to normal! No one knows who you are! Yay!" He gleefully danced around.

I couldn't help but laugh. As usual, he was right. For the first time in a long time, I was happy to be a nobody. In fact, I would take Weirdest forever if it meant I had my dad and my one true friend. I was so happy that a small burst of rainbows flew from my arms as I waved them around. Luckily, by that time, all the students were busy with the emergency-service crews that were giving them clean bills of health, so no one noticed.

"Well, if it isn't the old career killer," Ms. Watson said as she walked over and laid eyes on Dad.

"Conspiracy nut," Dad growled at her.

"Yeah, obviously." She pointed at the destruction all around us. "Am I wrong?"

"Good point," Dad conceded.

"Where's my mom?" I asked her.

"I sent her home, with a very stern warning," Ms. Watson said.

"But what if she tells people about my powers?"

Ms. Watson snorted. "Who's gonna believe her? I had a badge, and for fifteen years no one ever believed me."

"We don't have to worry about you?" Dad asked.

She thought for a minute. "Listen," she said. "I'll make a deal with you. I want to stay a guidance counselor, and I'm sure you want to stay off the radar. Let's agree to keep this mystery unsolved. Indefinitely."

"Why?" I asked.

Ms. Watson sighed like I was asking her deepest, darkest secret. "Okay. Honestly, those paper pushers never appreciated me or my passion for fairness. These kids do. All they want is to be treated fairly, and I respect that. I'm staying here."

Without blowing her cover, Ms. Watson was still able to take over the situation (which had now been classified as a mild natural disaster) and keep the cops, reporters, and screaming PTA moms at bay. Once the last siren whooped away, it was actually quite peaceful in the hollowed-out shell of the gym.

"I'll see you two in my office on Monday morning," Ms. Watson said, pointing at Charlie and me as she climbed into her black SUV.

"Hey, I still have a few questions for you, lady," Dad said.

"As I do for you, Mr. McGowan."

"It's Rik. Do you have a first name or is that classified?"

"Get in the car, meathead, and we'll discuss over pie." She rolled her eyes before shutting the door.

"You okay, kiddo?" Dad asked me. "Wanna go home?"

I shook my head. "Not yet."

"You'll walk her home, Charlieman?"

"Yeah, of course, but I think you've got it backward—I need her protection," Charlie said. "It's late! There could be all sorts of weirdos out there. I want to be with the biggest one."

"Damn straight," Dad said proudly as he gave me a hug.

He and Ms. Watson took off with a merry little honk good-bye. I was pretty sure the horn played "La Cucaracha." What a freaking bizarro night.

"Well, that was all a bit surreal," I said. "And you know what the most mind-blowing thing is?"

"What?" Charlie asked.

"I think Ted was right. Like, he was trying to tell me about all of this."

"Strange days," Charlie agreed.

I took a big sip from a bottle of water one of the EMTs left. I had one more important thing I needed to say. "I'm sorry, Charlie. For everything, but mostly for being so dumb. You're my best friend. The only friend that really matters."

"It's cool," he started. "Well, it was horrible, but it's cool. I could've handled things with a bit more class."

We sat for another minute in silence, and it felt really good. It seemed like it had been forever since I had just sat and wasn't scared or nervous. "I'm glad I don't have to hide anymore. Well, not from my dad, at least."

"Wait!" Charlie said. "Speaking of hiding—did you see Betsy? She wasn't at the dance! Your powers wouldn't have hit her. She'll remember everything!"

I laughed in sheer amazement. "Oddly enough, Betsy is the one person I'm not worried about."

Charlie frowned, then shrugged, looking convinced.

Then he grandly bowed and offered me his hand. "We could dance."

"But there isn't any music."

"I know." Charlie took my hand. "And we are in a destroyed gymnasium and you have superpowers. I think we can wing it."

"True," I said.

We started to sway.

"Besides," Charlie added, "this is the Spring Formal, and I want to dance with an Est."

Even though my initial reaction was to pinch Charlie hard for that comment, he was right. I was an Est. I was Weirdest.

Maybe that wasn't what I'd wanted, but it is what I am. And I was starting to believe that wasn't so bad after all.

*Weird is wonderful.*

# Acknowledgments

Endless thanks to . . .

Tom and Dolly Nuhfer for their unflinching support of my weird job.

Paul Morrissey, who always helps, even when I don't deserve it.

Publishing genius (and fashion icon) Erin Stein for making it all happen.

Bernadette Baker-Baughman, who keeps me sane and safe through the ups and downs.

John Morgan and the entire Imprint crew for their excitement and hard work.

The brilliant and incomparable Katie Strickland, who should always be thanked.

# About the Author

Heather Nuhfer was born near the Allegheny Mountains in Pennsylvania, where, from the safety of her bedroom, she wrote stories featuring her own monsters.

While working at the Jim Henson Company, Heather finally met many creatures face-to-face, including the lovable characters of Fraggle Rock. Heather scripted the lead story in Henson's Harvey Award–nominated Fraggle Rock graphic novel series, and she is the author of several My Little Pony: Friendship Is Magic graphic novels. She's also penned stories for *Wonder Woman, Teen Titans Go!, The Simpsons, Scooby Doo*, and *Monster High*, and her episodes of Hasbro's *Littlest Pet Shop* are set to air in 2018. *My So-Called Superpowers* is her first novel.

When she isn't writing, Heather loves to knit while watching bad 1990s action movies with her furbaby, Einstein.